Eliza

St. Olave's

Vol. II

SALZWASSER
VERLAG

Eliza Stephenson

St. Olave's

Vol. II

Reprint of the original, first published in 1863.

1st Edition 2022 | ISBN: 978-3-37500-194-0

Verlag (Publisher): Salzwasser Verlag GmbH, Zeilweg 44, 60439 Frankfurt, Deutschland
Vertretungsberechtigt (Authorized to represent): E. Roepke, Zeilweg 44, 60439 Frankfurt, Deutschland
Druck (Print): Books on Demand GmbH, In de Tarpen 42, 22848 Norderstedt, Deutschland

ST. OLAVE'S.

VOL. II.

ST. OLAVE'S.

'Live for to-day ! to-morrow's light
To-morrow's cares shall bring to sight,
Go, sleep like closing flowers at night,
And Heaven thy morn will bless."

IN THREE VOLUMES.

VOL II.

LONDON

1863.

ST. OLAVE'S.

CHAPTER I.

THE day after the pic-nic was hot and drowsy. Grey in the sunshine stood the old Cathedral, idle shadows creeping round about within its lichened buttresses and over the carved work of the battlements and statue niches. The great west doors were flung wide open, revealing long shadowy ranges of clustered columns over which stray gleams of light from the many-coloured windows wandered to and fro. And often some passer-by, weary of the heat and sunshine outside, turned into the dim half-dark nave; just as at other times, when tired of life's glare and beating heat, he might turn for shelter into the cool haunted aisles of Memory.

Not a breath of wind stirred the goldening elm-trees. The prisoned spirit, whoever he might be, that wailed so often from the belfry tower, was silent this afternoon. The rooks swooped idly round and round the crocketed spires, or clustered high up on the battlements of the broad tower, cawing in sedate ecclesiastical monotone as though they were performing a cathedral service for their own special edification. Sometimes a misanthropic member of the company would wheel away by himself to the elm trees, and then, shaken off by the touch of his black wing, leaf after leaf fluttered noiselessly down, and nestled in the tall rank grass beneath. A group of little chorister boys, with very dirty collars and no wristbands to speak of, were playing marbles under the west door, one of their number being placed by turns as sentinel to give notice if the Dean or Canon-Resident should pass that way; for games of all sorts, especially marbles and hop-scotch, were strictly forbidden in the Close.

The warm pleasant day had brought out most of the almsfolk. Martin Speller looked blander than usual. He was sitting in his arm-chair outside his own cottage door, smoking his pipe and meditating sometimes on the blue-grey Minster towers, whose shadows stretched quite out to the almshouses, sometimes on the stray flies which were buzzing about on a voyage of discovery over his worsted stockings. Mrs. Marris could not indulge herself in the luxury of meditation this afternoon, for she was busy over a batch of short cakes, whose fragrant memorial wafted now and then from her oven door quite up to Martin Speller's chair, and made the old man snuff the air in an inquiring manner.

Mrs. Marris was anxious to get her cakes baked and eaten too, before the bell put in for afternoon prayers. She was free to confess those prayers put her sadly out of the way sometimes. They were very good, certainly, but she thought somehow folks needn't say them quite so often.

"'Pears like to me," she remarked to Mrs. Cromarty, who was standing outside the doorway with a basket of clean clothes for the Old Lodge, "'pears like to me, if folks says their Colic, and 'I believe,' reglar of a mornin, an' then uses their best endeavours to keep theirselves decent and not do no harm to no one, such a sight o' prayers ain't no yield much. Prayers is all right for them as hasn't got no cooking to do, but it don't stand to reason as folks can give their intellects to t' Litany, and do their reverences proper when they're wondering all t' while if t' pot's boilin' over, and if t' loaf wants turnin'. Leastways, that's my experience."

"But come yer ways in, Mrs. Cromarty, and sit ye down. I lay ye're pretty nigh beat out wi' this pec-nic."

"Ay, marry," said Mrs. Cromarty, roughly, and yet good-naturedly, "what wi' worretin' about to see as things didn't get broke—it 'ud go to my heart if yon white chaney of Mistress Grey's came to harm—an' then wi' washin' and fettlin' up afterwards, I reckon I'm pretty nigh sold up this time, anyhow."

"That's just it," and Mrs. Morris took the cake tin out of the oven with her apron, and turned over the rich brown cakes, "big folks does the pleasurin', and middle sized folks look at 'em, an' little folks, like you an' me, has to tew about and fend for 'em both. That's way things goes i' this here world, Mrs. Cromarty."

"Why, as for pleasurin', pec-nics ain't no great yield accordin' to my line o' thinkin'. It beats me, it does, Mrs. Marris, the trouble quality takes to make theirselves uncomfortable."

"Law, Mrs. Cromarty, what d'ye mean?" said Mrs. Morris, who was at a loss to comprehend this bold statement.

"Why, look here," and Mrs. Cromarty untied her bonnet strings, for she was getting warm, "when folks might hev' their dinner like Christians, off a decent meogny table, wi' reg'lar chairs, n' napkins, n' knives n' forks, n' things enough to set up a shop, besides glass n' chaney, and them as fetches an' carries, I don't see no manner o' sense in squattin' round a table-cloth as ain't got nothin' under it but grass and spiders, n' sich things. An' then, i'stead o' velvet cushions, same as they're used to at home, they'll sit 'em down wi' nowt but a bit o' shawl betwixt them an' t' grass, or mebby leanin' up agin an ould tree stum as gives 'em rheumatiz its so damp, let alone ants an' earwigs, an' beetles, an' things as lives in it, creepin' round an' crawlin' up ye."

Mrs. Marris shrugged her shoulders and shook out her lilac print gown.

"And then if it's a fine day, t' midges flies about and tumbles into t' chicken sass; an' if it's wet, rain splashes into t' open tarts and mashes 'em all to nothin', an' happen if it's been a bit damp the night afore, frogs starts hoppin' about and makin' t' young leddies skree out like mad. And then the waste, law, Mrs. Marris, the waste, why it 'ud make a heathen cry shame on 'em, to think o' the pies as gets upset, and fowls wi' white sass as tumbles promiscus among tarts an' cheesecakes, an' spoils 'em all; an' then, as likely as not, when you've got things put out as decent and christian as ye can, t' wind sets on—it's allers windy at a pec-nic— and mustard pot rolls right away into t' middle o' the custards, wi' the salt after it. It's unreasonable, Mrs. Marris, it is," and Mrs. Cromarty looked disgusted.

"'Tisn't vittles as lies on my mind," replied Mrs. Marris, "them as pays for 'em has a right to waste 'em if they've a likin' to, and t' money's into shopkeeper's pockets if it's out o' some one else's. But it's the way the dresses gets abused as riles *me,* Mrs. Cromarty. Now there's yon beautiful muslin as took me nigh upon half a day nobbut last week to do up for Miss Somers, and she's sent it back this mornin' wi' no more shape nor if you'd taken a yellow butterfly's wing and crunched it up i' yer hand. It's that sort o' waste as isn't seemly for folks as calls theirselves Christians; but I lay it 'ud be a viewly sight, Mrs. Cromarty, to see t' young leddies."

"Ay, they were rare an' menseful. It were kind o' witchin' to see 'em dancing afore they went off, they minded me o' nothing but bits o' cloud wi' sunlight shinin' on 'em, a flickerin' up an' down. Miss Alice was bonniest of 'em all though, she was i' white muslin wi' green spots."

"Ay, she's that sweet is Miss Alice, I could go down of my knees and say my prayers tull her a'most. I lay she'll no be Miss Alice long, there's over many young men comes spryin' round after her, and walkin' her out; but, law, there's my cakes burnin'; folks had ought to live wi' their heads inside t' oven door when they're bakin', or things is sure to catch."

"I'se seed our new trac' lady's brother," continued Mrs. Marris, as she overhauled her cake tin again, and turned its contents, "him, you know, as plays music at Minster, back'ards and for'ards this good bit past. Folks as goes to the Old Lodge allers has to come by my door, and

I've took heed of him pretty oft. D'ye think he's looking sweet upon her?"

"She'll none marry him, Mrs. Marris, she'll none marry him. She kind o' looks up tull him and he has t' rule over her just as if she were a baby. I've heerd him take her up right sharp sometimes, an' she never gives him so much as a word back; but she'll none marry him. She's that dainty, is Miss Alice, as she must hev' somebody that's gainly lookin' and pickish to match her. She'll none wed grey hairs and stoopin' shoulders."

"An' she's in t' right on it, Mrs. Cromarty. Viewly men and viewly women does best together. I ain't patience when a young lady what's as neat and jimp as a canary bird, goes an' weds herself to a man as looks like nowt but a sack o' flour wi' a string tied round its middle."

"Good looks is nobbut skin deep, and a fair face covers a false 'eart, and rosy cheeks turns to dust and ashes," ejaculated Betsy Dowlie, an almswoman from the other end of the row, who had come out to feel the sun, and was drawn towards Mrs. Marris's door by the increasing odour of the hot cakes.

Betsey Dowlie was a spare-looking woman of sixty-five or thereabouts. There was nothing remarkable about her appearance, save that her unstarched cap borders flimped up and down in a loose, purposeless sort of way, and the reverse aspect of her gown was generally unprepossessing, in consequence of a chronic disarrangement amongst its fastenings. She belonged to the same denomination as Mrs. Cromarty; but the two women had little in common except the bench on which they sat at the meeting-house, and were as unlike each other as the rosy-cheeked October apple is to its lean and shrivelled relative which has been gathered six months and kept through the frost and blight of winter-time.

From her seventh until her fourteenth year, Mistress Dowlie had been "taken in and done for" at the St. Olave's charity-school. At the completion of her educational curriculum, she was placed out with a batch of other girls in respectable service, and, being a quiet, washed-out, well-conducted sort of young person, she had given general satisfaction to her employers. Some ten or twelve years ago, the Dean and Chapter put her into one of the almshouses, with full possession of all the rights and privileges pertaining thereunto. A few of the families with whom she had lived, kept her in green tea, lump sugar, and sundry other spinster luxuries, so that, on the whole, pensioner No. 8 might be said to make a pleasant thing of life.

Most people would have contrived to erect a little edifice of thanksgiving on this solid foundation of creature comforts; but, unfortunately, Mistress Dowlie had a natural inaptitude for looking on the bright side of things. She was, like many other people, born into the world with drab spectacles on her nose, and had never been able to cast them. She was much given to abusing the present estate of life. According to her representation, it was a vale of tears, a waste howling wilderness, a thorny path which neither green tea at six shillings a pound, nor lump sugar *ad infinitum*, nor an allowance of nine shillings a week, could in any degree smooth or lighten. Listening to her description of it, one might have concluded that the world was a huge house of correction, and human bodies divinely appointed tread-mills for the unfortunate souls who were destined to inhabit them. A theological writer would have described her religious character as vehemently "*subjective,*" that is, she was more inclined to the inward grace of silence and meditation than to the outward one of keeping herself and her cottage bright and clean and trim.

"Hould your whisht, Missis Dowlie," said Mrs. Cromarty, it always made her feel as she expressed it, "kind o' aggravated," when her fellow-member began to launch out into animadversions on people and things in general. "Where's the need o' runnin' down God's good gifts and revilin' things as He's seen good to bless?"

"I aint sayin' nothin' but what's in t' Book, Mrs. Cromarty. What does Solomon say about favour an' beauty? Ye're wise enough if ye know more nor he did."

"I don't go for to say but what Solomon hisself liked a pretty woman better nor a plain un, nobbut she had discretion along with it. An' look at Queen Esther, warn't she fair 'n beautiful, an' didn't she put on her royal apparel when she went in to t' king, which, as I take it, means that she made herself look as menseful as she could, same as Miss Alice, bless her, does when she gets her white muslin and blue ribbons. I ain't patience wi' folks as can't let other folks be pretty, just 'cause their own faces is as ungainly as a black crow. I ain't to call comely mysel', but I allers likes to look at them as is."

Mistress Dowlie, beaten out of this line of thought, betook herself to another.

"Is yer experience prosperin', Mrs. Cromarty? It's a tryin' thing for folk's souls is livin' in t' midst o' so much gaiety. I mind when I were sittiwated ladies' maid wi' the Bishop's daughters, afore I came here, my sperittle feelins got awful thin an' weak wi' bein' so much agate over pomps and vanities."

"An they'll never be now't else but thin and weak, Mistress Dowlie, if ye're allers a tewin' an' scrattin' at 'em, to see how they're comin' on. Sperittle feelins is like starch things, less ye finger 'em an' better."

"Bless me, Mrs. Cromarty, you allers put things so queer-like. But surely folks had ought to know the state o' their minds, and whether they're in t' enjoyment o' grace or not."

"In course; but spryin' into yer feelins won't help ye on a bit. 'Tain't no yield axin' yerself how do ye feel, and what's state o' yer mind,— it's what are ye *doin'*, I allers axes. That settles t' question. When yer i' danger o' settlin' down into a low key, just start on an' ax the Almighty to show ye yer duty, an' what He's got for ye to do: an' when ye once get agate o' duty in His name, yer experience 'll spin along first-rate, without yer ever stoppin' to fix it up in t' right track."

"Well, I allers thought it were t' best way to get yourself cut off fra' outward things, an' shut yourself up an' meditate."

"Livin' out o' doors is healthier, Mistress Dowlie—livin' out o' doors is healthier. Bless ye, doin' yer duty's better nor a clothes-basketful o' t' best sperritle feelin's as was ever made."

"I ain't got no duties as I knows on," twittered Mistress Dowlie. "What mun I do?"

"Do, why do onything. Go down of yer knees and scrub that there floor of yours, while it shines again, and then brighten up yer pots and things, and then, if you've a bit o' time to spare, go an' read a psalm to yon poor ould blind woman as sits i' th' sunshine wi' sich a kind-like smile on her poor bit face. Bless ye, when yer sperittle experience starts o' runnin' thin an' weak, it's allers a sign yer missin' summmut as God Almighty's laid upo' yer conscience to mind."

Mistress Dowlie did not much relish this allusion to the state of her floor, and made no further effort towards keeping up the conversasion.

"Come now, both on ye," said Mrs. Marris, who never ventured into theological subjects, and had therefore been silent for the last few minutes, "You've been at it long enough, and prayers has got to come. Draw yer chairs up and have a bit o' tea. I allers likes to see folks comfortable."

Whilst the conversation had been going on, Mrs. Marris had brewed the tea and spread a cloth on the table. She now proceeded to cut up the cakes. Very tempting they looked,—crisp, richly browned, and well furnished with butter,—for when Mrs. Marris did give herself a bit of a treat, she had no notion of doing things by halves. Then she filled up the little black teapot, and called upon Mrs. Cromarty to say grace.

"I allers likes my tea," she said, after she had got through the first piece of short-cake; "it kind o' clears my intellects. Nobbut I'se forced to get it over soon, cause of the prayers. All t' summer time they goes in at half-past four, and there ain't time to hev' it comfortable. I've oft thought I'd get 'em sided out first, and hev' a cup o' tea afterwards, but laws! I should get impatient afore they was over. Them two or three as comes towards back end, 'ud be awful long if I were a waitin' for my tea all t' time they was agate, an' so I just keeps along in t' ould track."

"I'm feared yer prayers don't do ye much good, Mrs. Marris, if ye ain't no more enjoyment nor that in 'em."

"Good, Mrs. Cromarty! bless ye no. I never look to get no good from 'em; we has wa 'lowance ye see by account o' goin' reg'lar; but it ain't no sperittle good in no shape or way whatever as I sees. They're awful stiff, such a sight o' bowin' and scrapin' and flittin' up and down as beats me to find out what it means."

"I'm sometimes thinkin' Mrs. Marris, though I don't go for to say nowt agin' other folks' ways, we gets nearer t' throne o' grace at our little room down yonder at t' Low Gardens. Its beautiful and sweet whiles is the influence as seems to come about us there, though the singin' ain't nothin' partic'lar to speak on."

"Nearer, yes I reckon ye do, a pretty sight nearer. I were there a week or two back, and it seemed like to me Mrs. Cromarty them folks was in t' right track if any was. It were awful solemn while t' address were on, an' I could ha' fretted if there hadn't been such a sight o' people. But law Mrs. Cromarty! I were sort o' skeered when they started prayin'; they bawled that loud while I was feared them outside 'ud think summut was up."

"Folks can't allers trim their voices when they're in airnest. Mrs. Marris. They'd better bawl their prayers wi' a feelin' heart nor chant 'em to a tune without thinkin' what it is they're sayin'."

"Ye're in t' right on it, Mrs. Cromarty. Nobbut folks is sincere I don't matter ways and means; but it goes again me the way they does things at yon place of ours," and Mrs. Marris pointed with her cup in her hand to the Minster. She always spoke as if she had a personal and vested interest in St. Olave's Cathedral and its appurtenances.

"Them there little singin' lads has all manner of unproper freaks when t' prayers is agate. It were nobbut a bit since I seed two of 'em countin' out a bag o' marbles while they was on wi' the 'Lettest thou depart.' Now I don't put in to hev a great sight o' religion myself, but I was allers brought up to know what's proper, and I just gived 'em a look, but it warn't no yield, not a bit. Now Mrs. Cromarty, it's that sort o' thing oft trips me up and sets me thinkin' whether God Almighty makes an account o' such like prayin' an' praisin'."

"I lets these here things alone, Mrs. Marris; there's a vast o' things i' this world as the best you can do with 'em is to let 'em alone. They'll smother ye i' no time if ye start tewin' with 'em. Maybe the Lord sees good where poor mortals like us doesn't. Tain't clear to me as the blessed Apostles singed their prayers, but if book-larned folks thinks its the gainest way, why it ain't my track to find fault. Ye'll need to go and sort yourself, Mistress Dowlie; yon's bell puttin' in for prayers."

"I aint goin' to t' prayers," said Mistress Dowlie stretching herself, "I'se got a pain i' my inside. These cakes o' yourn is over rich, Mrs. Marris."

"Take a bit o' ginger, honey," and Mrs. Marris went to the corner cupboard, from which she took out a little bottle and put some of the contents into a cup. "Here's some, best sort, as Miss Bruce, bless her, gived me when I was badly fore-end o' t' year. There's nowt so good as a bit o' ginger for a pain i' the inside; it clears it off i' no time."

"Ay," said Mrs. Cromarty with a glance at Mistress Dowlie's somewhat cadaverous looking physiognomy, "an it 'll do yer sperittle feelins a vast o' good too, see if it won't; folks oft gets into a low key, and their experience clean runs to nothin', and they think they're goin' to be cast out straight away, when its nothin' but colic, and a bit o' ginger 'ud fix 'em upright and make 'em like giants refreshed wi' new wine."

Mistress Dowlie groaned, but took the ginger and then set off slowly towards her own door, her cap borders flapping about in a vague, undecided sort of way.

"It's nowt but meditatin' and meditatin' and meditatin'; there aint no yield in that sort o' thing," said Mrs. Cromarty when the subjective spinster was out of sight. "David said while he was agate o' musin' the fire burned, but I'se warrant it 'ud ha' gone out again sharp enough, if he hadn't tuned up and sung that blessed psalm to keep it in."

"Poor body," said Mrs. Marris, taking her black silk bonnet from the peg behind the door, "I allers pities them as can't get their talkin' done for want o' folks to listen to em'. There's yon poor Mrs. Edenall, as lives wi' Miss Bruce, I clean wearies for her, she looks so corked up like. She's as full o' trouble as she can hold, and she ain't got nobody to tell it to."

"Mrs. Edenall's a born queen," said Mrs. Cromarty. "She minds me o' that young leddy I telled ye of, ye rec'lect don't ye."

"Ay marry, I shan't let that story slip. Her as got beguiled away and never came back no more; image of Miss Alice you said she was."

"Whisht, Mrs. Marris, whisht. It goes agen' me to hear ye liken bonnie Miss Alice to yon poor lorn creetur' as ruined herself body and soul for him as didn't care the toss of a penny for her. But its the make o' Mrs. Edenall as minds me o' my poor leddy. She'd just that way with her like a princess, prideful and yet so sorrowful whiles, as if she'd gotten a look at things as had to come."

"Talk o' some folks an' you're sure to see 'em. There's Mrs. Edenall comin' up t' road; she passes here as reg'lar as clockwork of an afternoon to go to prayers. Law now, Mrs. Cromarty, isn't she a pictur' o' pride?" And the two women stood within the doorway to watch her.

She came along with a firm, deliberate tread, Cleopatra-like, slow and stately. Martin Speller took his pipe out of his mouth, uncrossed his legs, rose, and made a low creaky bow as she passed. She saw him preparing to accomplish this act of reverence, and put out her hand with a deprecating gesture,—who was she that any human creature should cringe to her? But it was too late, he was on his feet and the deed done before she could prevent it.

"I'd as soon do my obedience tull her as any of 'em," said Martin as he sat down, recrossed his worsted stockings, and put his pipe in his mouth. "She's a born leddy she is, I knows real quality when I sees 'em, same as I tells good bacca, and she's got the make of a queen in her, though folks hereabouts hasn't found it out."

Mrs. Marris and Mrs. Cromarty dropped a rustic curtsey as she passed them. Mrs. Edenall returned it gravely, quietly, almost humbly, with far more grace than she would have tendered to the Dean's lady or even the Bishop himself. Mrs. Cromarty stood at the door watching her until she disappeared behind the west front of the Cathedral. Then, taking her clothes basket, she walked slowly away up the narrow lane that led to the Old Lodge garden.

CHAPTER II.

JANET Bruce sat in the little parlour at Westwood waiting for David to come home.

The wind crept with a low sigh round and round the garden, sometimes sharpening almost into a scream, anon dying off into a dismal hopeless wail, and the rain-drops plashed heavily with slow monotonous drip, drip, from the vine leaves round the trellis.

Within, however, all was bright and pleasant. That parlour at Westwood always looked best when daylight was gone. Janet might keep out the sunlight with lattice-work of leaves and creeping plants, but she could not prevent the firelight from frisking merrily round as it did now, making quaint, flickering, changeable Chinese shadows on the white window blind, and gleaming with a soft, warm glow over the glazed paper, and bringing out into still bolder relief the fine old carved oak frame with its wild wealth of buds and flowers and winding arabesque work. The unlighted lamp stood on the table, and by it a vase of wild flowers,—forget-me-not, pimpernel, harebell,—with one or two golden wheat ears and a few feathery plumes of grass which Janet had gathered by the roadside as they came home from Norlands.

The timepiece was on the stroke of nine o'clock. Miss Bruce was not surprised at her brother being late. She took it for granted that Mistress Amiel Grey would ask him to go in and stay supper at the Old Lodge; and, once seated there, the rain would be likely enough to detain him, even if nothing else did.

To wile away the time, she had taken out, her knitting work—the little white sock which, like Penelope's web, seemed destined to perpetual unfinishedness. She looked just as tidy and peaceful and patient as ever, as she sat there, rocking to and fro in the great easy chair by the fire. Judging from the dainty neatness of her grey Llama dress, and the smooth, unwrinkled whiteness of her linen collar and cuffs—which might have been turned off Mrs. Cromarty's ironing-board scarce ten minutes before—no one would have thought that Janet had been all day pleasuring at a pic-nic. There was not even a touch of more than ordinary weariness on her face, nor a tinge of that dim twilight *ennui* that comes after the sunshine of pleasure. Few things stirred her spirit now out of that utter quietness which had become its settled habit.

Meanwhile David Bruce was making headway as best he could against rain and pain and—what is sometimes harder to bear than either—disappointment.

Indeed, the walk home from Norlands was not likely to be a pleasant one. It is, to say the least of it, wounding to a man's *amour propre*, to have his place at a lady's side usurped by one younger, handsomer, perhaps more agreeable than himself, and to be dropped half-way on the road as a useless worn-out thing of no further service or convenience. It requires a fair amount of dignity to go through such an experience with any sort of credit, or to look back upon it without a great smart of wounded vanity.

But David Bruce had that dignity. Deep down in the heart of him there was a quiet, unwavering self-appreciation—not self-esteem, though often confounded with it—which neither rose nor fell with passing circumstances. He knew himself for what he was, and could therefore afford that other people should sometimes mistake him. He had no vanity to be ruffled by failure, no self-conceit to be nipped and crushed by Mr. Cuthbert Scrymgeour's indifference or scorn. To a fussy little man, the humiliation of such an accident would have been intense, the mortification very keen. He would have fretted and pined over it all the rest of the way, and been in a bad temper for at least a month. David Bruce just walked on quietly and bravely, as if nothing had happened. All he lacked was that pleasant hopeful feeling which had made the beginning of the ride home so bright.

Before he had got half way, for he could not walk fast on account of his sprained wrist, that was becoming very painful, the rain came plashing down in great sullen drops, and black clouds rolled up from behind the Norlands hills. The first thought that came into David Bruce's mind when he saw them, was that Alice would be safely sheltered before the storm could break in its fury. He could bear it for himself so only it did not reach her. And indeed, she had been sitting for a full hour in the crimson-curtained Oriel room of the Old Lodge, before he arrived, chilled, drenched, and shivering, in the narrow lane which led up to Westwood.

Janet came to meet him in the hall, and looked amazed to see him standing there dripping like a diver.

"Oh, Davie, how wet you are! Surely Mrs. Grey could not have known how fast it is raining, or she would never have let you walk from the Old Lodge without an umbrella; she is always so thoughtful and kind."

Then her brother had to explain all; Benjie's miraculous performances, the upset against the bank, Mr. Scrymgeour's timely, or untimely appearance, and the story of his accident. But indeed the arm began to tell its own story, for it had swollen frightfully, and there would be no more organ-playing for David Bruce just yet at any rate.

Janet took off his dripping coat, and fetched the warm dressing-gown and slippers which had been waiting for him at the fire. Then she got him some hot coffee, and made him drink it whilst she bathed and bound his arm. If tender nursing could have supplied his need, David would lack nothing so long as that quiet-hearted sister was near him.

There was such pleasant soothing leisureliness in all Janet's household ways. What she did was done so quietly, so tenderly. She never fussed over anything or anybody, never sympathized loudly whilst she forgot to help. All the deep-lying goodness of her nature came out at the sight of pain. When things went brightly and merrily, Janet might be and very likely was, rather a dull companion. She had no wit to enliven, no ripple of jest or anecdote to freshen the tide of talk, no sparkling laugh to kindle its reflection in the face of those it met. She was still, almost too still for the happy time. But when sunshine was over and gone, when need, sorrow, sickness, or any other adversity came, then those who had to do with Janet Bruce felt the value of her patient, true-hearted kindness.

"You're very good, Jeanie. I wearied sair for

ye the night," said David, as he leaned back on the sofa and his sister sat by him with her knitting work. Often when these two were alone at home, they fell into their own tender old Scottish phrases, those phrases which seem to have so much more warmth and friendliness than our slippery English idioms.

Janet's face brightened as she heard him say this; it grew nearly beautiful. Her brother was all she had to live for, and his words of love were very precious. To feel that she could do him good, to feel that he looked to her in any way for comfort and tenderness, was all the happiness she had now, and it was all she needed. She laid down her work and put her hand into his.

"I think after all, Davie, home is the best place for us. The proud faces about here don't look kindly on us. I would not be ill-pleased never to see them again."

"We must e'en be content with ane anither for the noo, Jeanie," said David, quietly keeping her hand in his, but his voice did not sound quite so wearily as Janet's, though his face was very pale. The most of love and hope lay before him yet; for her it was all passed by, and the best she could do with life was to be patient with it.

"Jeanie," he said, after a long pause, in which the silence had been so deep that his voice falling upon it made her start. "Jeanie, how still the room feels."

"It's because Mrs. Edenall is away," Janet replied. "I don't know how it is, but wherever she is, there seems to be a sort of tumult. She gives me the feeling of a crowd, of being pressed upon and crushed. As soon as she is gone, the quietness comes back. This room has never been quite like its old self since that first night she came into it."

"You are growing fanciful, Jeanie; where is she now?"

"Oh, she took her lamp and went to bed more than an hour ago. She was very still after we came home from Norlands; at least I mean she did not speak at all, though she seemed to be in a sort of restless flutter."

"She would be tired, perhaps; you know she is not accustomed to much exercise, and you must have walked eight or nine miles to-day at the least."

"No, Davie, she wasn't tired, I'm quite sure of that. She was walking up and down the room the whole of the time after we came home, until she made me dazed and bewildered with the continual motion. Then she bade me good night and said she was going to bed, but Tibbie says she's not gone to bed, for she's heard her walking the room this hour past almost. Davie, she is a very strange woman."

"We will let her alone, Jeanie, and be tender to her. Her life has had some great wrench that she keeps from us. What she wants is rest, and we will try to give it her."

There was another long pause. This time Janet broke it.

"Brother, Alice Grey would like fine to ride home with Mr. Scrymgeour. She would be pleased with him."

David winced. There came over him that creeping, magnetic chill which we feel when we find that the thoughts of others, especially if they be sad and uncanny thoughts, have been going along in the same track as our own. He said somewhat sharply—

"Why? what makes you think that?"

Janet did not notice the sharpness, at any rate she did not heed it. She still kept David's hand in her's, and said in just her quiet matter-of-fact tones—

"Alice loves anything that is dainty and beautiful. It is in her nature, she cannot help it. You remember what she said this afternoon at Norlands about her ideal of a man."

David did remember it. But Janet unconsiously cleared off any purple haze of hope which the memory of those words of Alice's might have left, by putting the matter in the light of sober common-place reason.

"Girls, and especially warm-hearted impulsive girls, like Miss Grey, mostly fix upon those who are very opposite to the ideal they have set up in their own minds. She says she does not care for beauty and gracefulness; now Brother, I think that those two things are the things above all others that will really most sway her choice. It is always so. If you notice you will find it every day of your life. When a young girl professes a preference for one style of character, it is more than likely she will fix upon its very opposite."

David Bruce loosed his hold of Janet's hand,

and finding it at liberty she went on with her knitting work He looked across to the mirror. It revealed a shock of shaggy grey-black hair, falling untidily over a face very deeply furrowed with the hard lines of thought and endurance. In contrast with his sister's, quiet and placid and peaceful as a lake in the summer-time, there was still less of what people generally call beauty in it. Janet's eyes were bent down over her work, so that she did not see the almost defiant look that came into his.

He said no more just then. The straight even brows tightened into a rugged line, and the lips took a sterner bend. Janet thought once or twice she heard a sharp quick-drawn breath, but it might be only his arm that was paining him. By-and-by he murmured, as if tired and sleepy,

"Jeanie, after all the best part of a pic-nic is the coming home again."

And though the voice this time was not so bright, his sister was pleased to hear him say it.

CHAPTER III.

TIBBIE was quite right. That night had been no resting time for Mrs. Edenall.

When she went into her room she locked and bolted the door, and looked into the cupboards, pressing together the empty dresses that hung there to make sure that no one lurked behind them. This custom had grown into a habit with her during the long years of a life in which she had had no friend to care for or protect her. Then she wrapped herself in her scarlet dressing gown, and, drawing out an easy chair, sat down by the little table that stood in the window.

The sky was black with rain clouds, save in the

east, where they tore into ragged fringes through which the harvest moon peered with a faint uncertain glimmer, just serving to reveal the outline of the chesnut trees that bounded the garden, and beyond them the gabled roofs of the tall old-fashioned houses on the outskirts of the city. Mrs. Edenall turned away from these, and looked towards Norlands, thinking perhaps of the little coffin and the baby soul which had found sure rest so soon.

She must have sat there for nearly half-an-hour; then with a sigh she roused herself and drew towards her a desk that stood on the table. When she had unlocked this she took out of it a worn-out pocket-book, carefully wrapped in many folds of paper.

It was an unsightly looking thing, out of date for the last twenty years at least. On the faded morocco cover was a silver plate in the form of a shield, bearing the initials "D. R." It opened with two clasps, both very rusty now, and the inside was lined with rich silk of the Ramsay tartan, which, though dimmed and frayed, still showed the red stripes and checkers of black and white. There were but few leaves remaining in the book, and the entries that had once been made there seemed long ago blotted out by tears that had fallen upon them. These leaves were confined in their place by a silken band, so that year by year they might be taken out and supplied by fresh ones. Pressed between them were a few foreign flowers, a cluster of Alpine rose, two or three fern sprays, a single linden leaf—such trifles as young lovers cherish, and which, short-lived though they be, often last longer than the happy time that first made them precious.

She turned these over tenderly, as a mother might handle the playthings of her dead baby. Sometimes a low, rippling laugh, ending in a sigh, broke through her parted lips, and as she pressed her cheek to the withered things, a loving, human-natural look softened the keen outlines of her face. After these mildewed pages came a little pocket, fastened with a second silver clasp, bearing the same initials as the outer one. From this she took a folded paper. Opening it, there fell out upon her lap a single curl of strong bright flaxen hair, entwined with a long tress of golden brown. Inside the paper were these words, written in a man's hand:—

"Marian and Douglas. Under the linden trees of Bulach. August, 18—"

She unbound her own hair, and let it fall over her shoulders in great, massy waves. Then taking up the silken tress, she matched it with those fast greying locks from which the golden sheen had long ago faded. What memories were they that the idle task brought back? For as she did it, her face grew hard, and stern, and pale with the shadow of unforgotten wrongs. By-and-by she flung the paper from her lap, and began to pace the room, slowly at first, then quickly, impatiently; her hands sometimes tightly clenched together, sometimes outstretched as though to bid away some loathsome thing.

The Cathedral clock struck eleven. The Westwood people were late to-night, on account of the pic-nic. Soon after the bells had finished chiming, Tibbie's heavy tramp was heard on the stairs. Then the door of Miss Bruce's room closed, and all was quiet for the night.

Still Mrs. Edenall paced up and down, wildly, fiercely. At last she stopped, picked up the paper which she had awhile ago flung upon the floor, and bending over the lamp, held in its clear flame the two locks of hair, until they were burned to a cinder. With a strange, sardonic smile, she watched how they writhed and crackled and struggled in the heat, then dropped fragment by fragment, until nothing remained of them but a little heap of grey ash.

Nothing but that. No power of hers could bring back the golden lock now, either to speak of any wrong whose remembrance it had been, or to tell of dead joys, once as bright as its own sunny beauty. Perhaps she thought of this, for with the eagerness of a hasty, impulsive nature, she caught up the slip of paper which held the two names, and pressed it passionately to her lips. Over and over again she kissed it, leaning her cheek down upon the yellow faded writing, as if any love given now could charm back the treasure it had once kept for her.

Weary at last, she folded her arms on the table and buried her head in them. Once and again a deep sob broke the stillness of the room; once a solitary tear rolled down her cheek, and glistened over the great heavy waves of hair that lay loosely round her.

One after another the quarters struck from the

bell tower of St. Olave's, but still she crouched there mute and moveless, as though carved in stone. The stroke of one o'clock rang out, falling with a heavy resonant clang upon the hushed air. The rain poured fiercely upon the windows; the wind moaned round and round, blowing often in sudden, impatient gusts through the window-frames, and scattering over that prostrate form the grey ashes that still lay beneath the lamp.

When at last, after that dreary vigil, Mrs. Edenall rose, her face was very pale, but there was no longer any pride or passion in it,—any hope or human tenderness. It was the face of one for whom all outlook of earthly joy is passed away, before whom past and future are alike stretched as one flat, arid, ungreened wilderness. It was the face of one who bends no longer over the dying, but the dead; who has no longer any life to cherish, or any spark of hope to keep from fading out.

She had not the look of one who has prayed, and so, even in the utter darkness, won strength to grapple with despair; or of one who, treading the valley of death and feeling the chill wind blowing up its steeps, sees beyond them a rest that may hereafter be reached. No ray, not even the faintest, of that peace which God gives, glimmered from those weary eyes, or softened the rigid lines of the lips which were folded down in such passionless despair.

Good, happy, fireside women never see such faces, even in their dreams. But now and then the gleam of a policeman's lantern flashes upon them as they peer out livid and ghastly from the slime of Adelphi arches, after the poor souls that once looked through them have shivered into eternity. And it may be that Sabbath after Sabbath, when beneath cathedral roofs, and from softly cushioned pews, the prayer goes up for "all who are desolate and oppressed," Christ, the Pitiful, the Merciful One, remembers such as these, and prays the Father for them.

And all the time, close to this silent suffering woman, so near that they could almost hear each other's breath, Janet Bruce slept quietly on, knowing none of these things.

CHAPTER IV.

LITTLE by little grey morning crept up above the eastern sky. Wave after wave began to curl and ripple over the infinite ocean of sleep, and as it broke upon the shore of waking life, tossed itself into those wreaths of foamy fantastic spray which we call dreams.

Alice Grey woke in the midst of a rambling vision. She was in a beautiful Highland glen, whose sides were clothed with tall pine trees, and tangled with clasping fern and long tresses of white-veined ivy. From the rocks at one end gushed out a little cascade, widening as it descended until it flowed through the valley beyond in a broad stream. She was on one side of this stream and David Bruce on the other. He wanted to join her, but the water was too deep, and they both walked on separately to the source of the stream, where it narrowed into a little runnel which a child might ford. He came to her then, and was just going to clasp her hand, when the waterfall suddenly shrunk into two tiny cataracts of wavy light-brown hair, over which the rocks and trees shaped themselves into the chiselled face and crisp curly locks of Mr. Cuthbert Scrymgeour. Here David vanished away, and with that Alice woke.

The sun was shining bravely in through the window. The first thing that it showed her was her muslin dress, crumpled up in a heap on one of the chairs, and doing its best to bear out the correctness of the simile which Mrs. Marris had used. One or two wheat ears were still clinging to it. The sight of them brought back the whole affair of the pic-nic, and then for the first time since she came home, Alice thought of David Bruce, and wondered how he was getting on—whether his arm had really been much hurt, and whether he had got very wet in walking home from Norlands after she had left him.

She got up and laid the wheat ears carefully away in a drawer. Her heart smote her rather for having been so forgetful. She would go the first thing when breakfast was over, and ask how he was. Or stay, not so; she would go to the Minster first, and hear if he played the organ; she should know his touch she was quite sure. If he did play, all would be right, and she need not trouble herself, if he did not, she would go straight away to Westwood and see him. Possibly, though Alice did not ask herself the question, the chance of Mr. Scrymgeour reading prayers at the Minster had something to do with this determination.

Aunt Amiel did not come down to breakfast. She scarcely ever left her room now until ten or eleven o'clock, for she was growing very infirm. Alice took her a cup of coffee upstairs and sat by her whilst she drank it, amusing the old lady meanwhile by a full account of the pic-nic, the walk to Norlands, the climb to the top of the tower, the dance in the garden; and then, for the second time, the adventure which befel them on the road home. Whilst she was relating it, the bells began to chime for morning service, and before she had got as far as Mr. Cuthbert Scrymgeour's sudden apparition, she had to run away and put on her hat and scarf.

Mistress Amiel Grey's seat was at the organ end of the choir, next to the Deanery pew and the stall of the resident Canon. It commanded a first-rate view of the congregation, if that was any advantage, being somewhat elevated and facing the whole range of seats away down to the altar-screen. Most of the people had come in when Alice got there, and she walked up the aisle with a pleased fluttering consciousness that perhaps Mr. Scrymgeour might be watching her from his aunt's pew. She was mistaken though, for when she rose from her preliminary devotions and glanced shyly in that direction, the crimson curtained enclosure just beneath the Bishop's seat of state was unoccupied save by the rustling black draperies of the Archdeacon's widow.

The almshouse people were in their places on one of the front forms near the reading-desk, close under the vigilant eye of the Canon, who checked any incipient signs of sleepiness by a look that spoke unutterable things. Mrs. Marris's lilac gown was bginning to stand in need of the kindly offices of the wash-tub; it had been put clean on last Sunday morning, and the week was now wearing to a close. Perhaps, according to her own philosophy, this fact might account for her not enjoying the prayers so much this morning, for she evidently found it difficult to keep awake, and her leather-covered Prayer-book tottered suspiciously before the Litany was half over. Next to her sat Martin Speller, a *cui bono* sort of look on his shrewd hard-lined face, as if he were perpetually saying to himself "Prayin' aint no yield as ever I see." Betsy Dowlie was there too, with her flapping cap borders and coal-scuttle bonnet, and at the end of the bench sat Ruth Cane, her sightless face turned towards the organ, that face whose sunshine never died out and whose calm no storm had leave to break.

By-and-by the crimson curtains parted and a milky river of surplices flowed into the choir, dividing into two smaller streams which poured into the choristers' pews on each side. Then came the Dean, a tall stately man with scarlet hood and tasselled cap, and Dr. Hewlett, one of the sub-Canons, whose grand, peaceful face seemed like—

> "the benediction
> That follows after prayer."

Next entered the officiating clergymen. Alice glanced furtively at them under her long eyelashes, hoping that one might be Cuthbert Scrymgeour; but again she was destined to be disappointed. One was young Mr. Grace, the vicar-choral; the other Dr. Stern, a short stout man with an extensive tract of stubby hair shooting down into a peninsula of whisker on each side his rubicund cheeks.

When all had reached their places they knelt down. The little singing-boys covered their heads with their surplices and were understood to go through a prayer, but judging from a stray waft of peppermint and black-jack which came from that locality, it is to be presumed they were regaling themselves with something more earthly and sensual. The great Cathedral bell struck ten, and when the last stroke had died away, the service began.

Alice looked up into the organ gallery; the curtain was closely drawn this morning, and she could not tell whether the piece of head which now and then rose above it, belonged to Mr. Bruce or not. The first notes of the organ, however, in the "Venite," convinced her that he was not there.

That grand old instrument was like a high-mettled steed, docile as a child under the guidance of a powerful hand, obedient to the slightest touch which came with the ring of authority; but utterly fractious and unmanageable for the venturesome fingers of an amateur. The notes came tumbling out in glorious confusion, now rolling along in magnificent defiance of the unpractised hand that vainly attempted to guide them, and now breaking off into spasmodic squeaks and jerks which ruined the gravity of the little singing-boys, and made the grown-up choristers look profoundly disgusted. The discord grew worse and worse; at last, the Dean signed to the verger, who took a message into the organ-gallery, whereupon the instrumental part of the performance came to an untimely conclusion.

Alice wearied for the service to be over. The prayers and lessons had never seemed so long before. There was no melody in the voice that read them, and she had not yet learned to find any music in the words beyond that which the speaker could give. When the last Amen was over, she slipped away through a little side door at the north end, and past the trim, high, old-fashioned

Close houses into the secluded road that led to Westwood.

She found them all at home. Mrs. Edenall was sitting in the window-seat, a little paler than usual perhaps, but with that same drawn, rigid look about her face which it always wore when she was not alone. She had a piece of netting in her hand, the first work of any kind Alice had ever seen her do. She laboured on at it mechanically, scarcely ever looking at it though, but peering out into the garden with the same far-off unconscious gaze that Alice remembered the first time she had met her. She returned the young girl's greeting with a vague sort of stateliness, that had neither recognition nor friendship in it, and then went back to her seat.

Alice's better self was always in the ascendant when she entered the parlour at Westwood. Some rooms appear to have a perpetual consecration belonging to them. Crossing their thresholds it seems as natural to pray as though the lofty aisles of a cathedral bent over our heads, and the solemn tones of its worshippers were sounding in our ears. There is a feeling of sacredness in the air, a silent indefinable presence of something which wakens from our sleeping hearts that which is best and holiest. There are homes in this land of ours, more hallowed by the lofty, unconscious, ever-present influence of Christian character, more enshrined by the benediction of Him whose altar is the faithful heart, more instinct with unspoken prayers, more fragrant with the incense of charity, than many a church whose marble pavement and fretted roof have been made holy ground by a bishop's outstretched hands.

Alice's vain thoughts fell away from her. Quick to take on every passing influence, she became grave, silent, subdued. The shy, reverent look stole into her face which always came there in the presence of those she could honour and trust. It made her seem very beautiful.

Mr. Bruce was sitting by the table before a pile of manuscripts. The music of his Oratorio was finished now, and for the last week or two he had been writing out the separate voice parts for the singers in London who had undertaken its first performance. Janet was kneeling by his side; he was trying to instruct her how to copy out the parts. She had no taste for music; but if loving patience could accomplish the task, she had enough of that and to spare. She looked very bewildered though, as her brother explained to her the various terms, the unmeaning signs and foreign expressions which had to be used.

Alice saw at a glance what was needed, and, without waiting to get through any previous hand-shakings or inquiries, proffered assistance.

"Ah, Mr. Bruce, let me take some of these, and copy them out for you. I have nothing to do now, and I should be so glad to help you."

David looked up. Just the frank, eager, girlish face met him which had bent over those musty old folios in the organ pew, and the little hands were outstretched as if restless for something to do.

"You never heard me come in, did you? you and Miss Bruce were so busy over your papers, and I didn't have to ring the bell because Tibbie was in the hall. How is that arm of yours?" she continued, as she fluttered down to a foot-stool beside him and laid her hand with a gentle clinging touch upon his, which was in a sling. Her fingers felt cool, and soft, and velvety, like young geranium leaves which children rub against their cheeks, and there was that pretty half-pitying, half-wistful look in her face.

"It's only a sprain," David replied, "and I suppose it is going on well enough, but the surgeon says I must not go near the organ again for a month at the least, so I had to send to the Deanery and ask them to provide a substitute. Have you been at the prayers this morning?"

"Yes, indeed, and a marvellous performance it was. I assure you Benjie's antics were nothing in comparison," and Alice laughed outright at the remembrance of it.

"Ah," said David, playing with the little fingers that still rested on his arm, "my organ is frisky with any one who does not know how to manage it. It wants humouring, and likes to have its own way very much."

"It got its own way this morning, at any rate. The music reminded me of a kitten walking over the keys of a piano. But they only got so far as the 'Venite,' and then the Dean sent up a message, and we had no more of it."

"A good riddance. I wonder who it was that played."

"Some conceited elf no doubt—but William Tell's bow was too much for him. It will make the Dean and Chapter value your services all the more, Mr. Bruce; and now tell me what I can do with this music?" And Alice got up and began to turn over the loose sheets which were lying in confusion upon the table.

"Are you sure you understand copying? you know a few false notes may blast my reputation and drift me away into the waste howling wilderness of oblivion," said David merrily. Alice's presence made him feel gay-hearted again.

"I think you may trust me," she answered. "I used sometimes to copy for the organist we had before your time; he was my music master, and he told me a professional could not have done it better. You know," she added, "there is no one here to sing my praises for me, so I am obliged to sound them myself."

David set her to work upon a solo for a soprano voice. He did not tell her so, but it had been composed for her, and her own clear, pure, silvery tones had been ringing in his ears whilst he wrote it. He soon perceived from her manner of setting about the copying, that she was quite up to the mark in what she had undertaken. There was a beautiful daintiness and neatness in all that Alice did, together with a sort of fairy-like precision and dexterity.

"I knew very well you didn't think I could do it," she said, in reply to some remark David Bruce made as he bent over her, and watched her deft fingers gliding along the page. "But I am cleverer than you thought. I learned how to copy music a long time ago."

"Who taught you?"

"An old Scotchman who lived in the College Yard here, and got a living by doing the copying for the Minster. He was a queer funny old stick of a man, and had once been precentor of the Kirk of Auchterarder."

"Where?" said David, looking at her curiously.

"At Auchterarder, a town in Scotland. Don't you know it, it is on the road from Edinburgh to Perth."

"Yes, I know it well enough," David replied, "I suppose most Scotch folks ken Auchterarder; but I asked you to repeat it because I wanted to hear your pronunciation of the word. Say it again."

She said it again, giving with complete northern

accent the unspellable, German-like click of the "ch," and the rich, round, ringing sound of the "r's."

"Miss Grey has the genuine Caledonian speech, hasn't she, Janet? A veritable citizen of Auld Reekie could not say that word better."

Mrs. Edenall turned sharply round from her work, and looked Alice full in the face, but said nothing.

"I'm sure you must have Scottish blood in your veins," David continued. "I never met with an English person yet who was able to pronounce the name of that place. Let Mrs. Edenall try and you will soon see the difference."

Mrs. Edenall tried. She pronounced the "ch" as all English people do, as if it had been a "k." She made one or two more attempts, and then said impatiently, almost angrily—

"No, no, your unmeaning jargon breaks my throat. I will not try again."

Then Alice said the word, and the difference was perceptible enough. She turned round with a merry laugh to triumph over Mrs. Edenall.

But Mrs. Edenall had left the room.

"I don't know, I am sure, that I have any

Scottish blood in my veins. I'll ask Aunt Amiel about it. I remember though, when I was learning German, my master told me I managed the gutterals better than most of his pupils, but I thought he only told me it to please me. He was such a flatterer. He would tell people almost anything to make them like him."

And then they got into a discussion as to the truth of the oft-asserted fact that Scottish people pronounce the French and German languages better than their Southern neighbours. Whilst they were in the midst of the argument, Alice remembered that possibly Mr. Scrymgeour might be calling at the Old Lodge that morning, according to promise, and she did not want to be away when he came.

"I must go now," she said, gathering up the sheets of music which lay scattered on the table, and a roll of manuscript paper. She held out her hand to David Bruce to shake hands with him, and then remembering that his right hand was crippled, she took the other and retained it for a while in both of hers.

"When I have finished copying these, I shall come again and again for more until your wrist is quite well. I am so glad that I can help you at all."

With these words she fluttered away out of the room. When she was gone, all was still and quiet again. It was as if from some web of sombre texture, one solitary shining streak of gold had been suddenly removed.

David Bruce turned round to the fire, and shaded his face with his left hand. Janet, freed now from the incubus of the music copying, took up her knitting and set to work with quiet energy.

"What a sunshiny little creature Alice Grey is," she said after a while. "I should miss her so much if she were to go away from us now. Shouldn't you, brother Davie?"

No reply. She thought he had gone to sleep, for she knew he was very tired.

CHAPTER V.

"HAS anyone called, Masters, whilst have been away?" said Alice to the servant when she returned to the Old Lodge.

"No, Miss; only Captain Madden and Mr. Fleetwood have left cards. O yes, I beg pardon, Miss, Major Conway and Miss Somers called, but they did not come in."

"Anyone else?"

"No, Miss, that is all."

Alice left the music on the hall table and wen through into the garden, for she wanted some flowers to fill the dining-room vases. She had been busy all that week thinking about and preparing for the pic-nic, and they had got into rather a disordered state.

She found plenty of choice amongst the rich full-tinted autumn blossoms. Most of the roses were gone, exeept a few clusters of white ones, but there were tall fuchsias with their long pendant coral-like bells, some of rich deep crimson, some almost white, some pink, with "petticoats," as Mrs. Marris oddly enough named the under petals, of soft bloomy violet. There were spikes of iris and clumps of heather, yellow, purple and red; and from the hothouse—into which, however, the gardener was loth to admit her, for he knew well how ruthlessly she spoiled its fragrant treasures—from the hothouse, clusters of regal geraniums and the pale pink wax-like bloom of American hydrangea, with tresses of maiden hair, and long green fronds of the antlered fern. From the gables of the Old Lodge she gathered broad, clear-cut vine leaves and trailing bands of ivy, to make a background for the brighter tints of the flowers.

She soon filled her hat, and then carrying them into the Oriel room, tumbled them out in a promiscuous heap at the feet of Aunt Amiel, who was sitting in her great easy chair by the window.

Mistress Amiel Grey was failing very fast. No one could help noting a perceptible change in her appearance between this September morning and that warm, drowsy July afternoon eight weeks ago, when she welcomed Janet Bruce in this same oriel room. Her face was getting thinner and paler, but that was not all. Very often now in talking, especially to strangers, she would pause, hesitate, forget what she was going to say, and then, after a moment or two, start afresh on quite a different subject. Once too—it was after she had had a severe attack of headache—she began to talk to Alice in a vague, rambling way about a little child that had been sent to her to be brought up. She described it minutely, its looks, its pretty winning ways, its sweet temper. Alice saw that she was wandering, but humoured her, and listened, until at last Aunt Amiel dropped off to sleep, and the next day she remembered nothing about it.

This was nearly a fortnight ago. Generally, however, she was quite collected, and the physician who attended her said that with care and quietness she might yet live some years. Alice was of a happy temperament, not prone to mix the troubles of to-morrow with the pleasures of to-day, so whilst she tended her aunt with gentle, loving care, she put far away from her the thought of the time when those tender offices must cease, and the kind, sweet old face be seen no more.

She fetched a great Parian marble vase out of the window, and when she had emptied out its faded contents, and put in fresh water, she sat down on the carpet by her aunt's side, and began to arrange her fragrant treasures.

It was an employment after Alice's own heart. She had a very accurate eye for form and colour, that might be seen by a glance at her own dress, which was always so graceful and artistically arranged, the colours so well placed and skilfully blended. She would spend hours sometimes in summer and early autumn time turning her own little sitting-room into a perfect bower of greenerie. There was a natural grace about her which sorted well with flowers, and she was always happiest when busy amongst them.

With practised skill, such as no artist could

have taught her, she blended and contrasted the tints, and placed each leaf in its natural fall. Every now and then she would bend her pretty head on one side, to take in the general effect, then make some little alteration in the arrangement; moving a crimson fuchsia when it came too near a scarlet geranium, putting in a deep purple iris to tone down the bright colouring of a japonica, parting brilliant shades with a sober tinted leaf or two, relieving here and there a mass of green with a single pure white rose. Round the outside she wove a cornice of vine and ivy leaves, with delicate sprays of jasmine to break their sharply-pencilled outline, and drooping over the sides she hung long tendrils of bindweed and plumy clusters of fern. Mistress Amiel Grey sat in the arm-chair, watching with a pleased, caressing sort of smile, how the light fingers glided in and out through the brilliant mass of colour.

"Aunt Amiel," she said, plucking out a head of scarlet verbena, and putting a white rose in its place, "what do you think Mr. Bruce told me this morning?—he said he was quite sure I had some Scottish blood in my veins, I pronounced the names of the places so well. I was telling him you know, about that old man from Auchterarder, who taught me how to copy music."

Aunt Amiel looked disturbed; a shade of anxiety passed over her smooth, placid face, and she said, with the slightest touch of hauteur in her voice :—

"I had rather Mr. Bruce had not mentioned anything of the sort to you. It was quite needless to have suggested such an idea,—quite needless. Perhaps some day when you are older——"

Aunt Amiel paused; there was a loud, fashionable knock at the door. The colour came into Alice's face; she knew who it was, and she began to think with dismay of the appearance she must present, surrounded by bits of stalk and leaves, her hat off, her hair in wild untidiness, her dress disarranged, for she had pressed through a perfect thicket of lilac bushes to get to some roses that grew over the arbour, and her hands not over clean with fingering the gnarled ivy stumps. However, it was too late to beat a retreat. The visitor, whoever he might be, would have got into the hall before she could dash across it and fly upstairs into her own room. So there she stood in the midst of her horticultural remains, a very pretty picture certainly of innocent confusion and perplexity.

Masters threw open the door, and Mr. Scrymgeour walked in. Alice's eyes were bent upon the floor, bnt she got a sidelong glance at the clearly-chiselled face, and saw that it was turned towards herself. Mr. Scrymgeour paid his respects with grave courtly deference to Aunt Amiel first, and then insisted on shaking hands with Alice, who was vainly endeavouring to keep her dirty fingers out of sight behind the folds of her dress.

"We have been transported from Palestine to Olympus," he whispered in the daintiest and most silver tones of that magic voice, which had already won the hearts of half the Close young ladies. "It is no longer Ruth but Flora herself who has left the gods and come down to men."

Alice understood the allusion to Palestine, but her classic lore was quite at fault in the matter of Olympus; it might be one of the Sandwich islands for anything she knew to the contrary. She could find no words to answer him, and just stood silent beneath the amused, critical glance of his cold eyes, pulling to pieces an unfortunate spray of fuchsia, and growing rosier and rosier, until at last he made some further allusion to Aurora and the blushes of the morn, which completely mystified her, and with the bright tears sparkling iu her eyes she dashed past him and flew away to her own room.

When she was gone, Mr. Scrymgeour took Mistress Amiel Grey in hand, and played off his fascinating conversational powers upon her. He had a very winning manner towards elderly people, it was so full of courtesy, and a certain high-bred respectfulness. Mrs. Grey was not the first old lady by very many who had remarked what a charming companion Mr. Cuthbert Scrymgeour was, and how highly favoured the Archdeacon's widow might consider herself in having her declining years sustained by a young man of such perfect amiability and considerateness.

"My aunt would have accompanied me this morning," he said, placing her card in Mrs Grey's. hand, "but visitors detained her at home, and I could not delay any longer to inquire after Miss Grey. I trust the slight misfortune of last evening has produced no ill effects. Indeed, I need scarcely ask the question, her blooming countenance speaks for itself."

"Alice is quite well, thank you, Mr. Scrymgeour. I don't think she is easily frightened by anything. Indeed she appears to have enjoyed the ride home exceedingly, and I must express my thanks to you again for taking charge of her. I am indebted to you very much."

There was a quiet courtliness in Mistress Amiel Grey's manner as she said this, a touch of that measured precision that characterized the gentlewoman of fifty years ago, and which is now completely swamped in the free and easy intercourse of social life.

"Pleasant old lady," thought Mr. Cuthbert to himself; "seems to belong to the last century school of manners. Suppose she'll be churchy, like most of the Close folks; we'll try that track." And upon this hypothesis, Mrs. Grey's visitor drew her out into a conversation touching the ordination which was to be held at the Cathedral in the course of a few weeks; and from that to priest's orders and church preferment and so on.

Mr. Scrymgeour was correct in his supposition. Mistress Amiel Grey was "churchy," that is, she had a friendly home-like feeling towards all ecclesiastical matters; most people have such a feeling whose whole life has been spent beneath the shadow of Minster towers. The wives and widows of Deans or other church dignitaries talk of chapters and confirmations, vestments and rubrics, conclaves and convocations, as naturally as a farmer's wife discusses her baskets of butter, or a cantatrice her sensation songs.

Mr. Scrymgeour found that he had got upon the right track, and talked of Cathedral matters with as much gravity as if, like one of the St. Olave's rooks, he had lived all his life beneath the battered gurgoyles that peered out from the Chapter House buttresses. They were in the midst of a very interesting discussion respecting the proper method of intoning the Litany, Mrs. Grey preferring the monotone used by the late Dean,—in which preference Mr. Scrymgeour perfectly agreed,—when Alice returned.

Unlike some young ladies, who when caught in their morning dishabille rush off promiscuously and return in the full splendour of afternoon toilette, Alice had too much good taste to change the simple dress in which Mr. Scrymgeour had found her. But she had smoothed her wealth of sunny curls, and got the flower stains from her fingers, and looked as bright and fresh as a daisy when she made her appearance again. The pretty colour was warm as ever in her cheeks too, when Cuthbert rose to bring a chair and asked her where she would like to sit.

"Not anywhere, thank you. I don't want to sit down at all. I must clear away these leaves," she said, looking towards the scattered carpet. Any employment which did not oblige her to raise her eyes suited Alice best just then.

"I am afraid you will think me sadly untidy, Mr. Scrymgeour, but I've been so busy all the week, I could not arrange my flowers before, and really those roses looked as if they were asking some one to rob them."

"Like some other roses that I know," he replied with a meaning glance that quite put to flight all poor Alice's little stock of composure, and made her glad to stoop down and begin to gather up the leaves and stalks to the great detriment of her newly washed hands. She scarcely knew what had come to her; she never felt in this nervous, fluttering, all-overish way when David

Bruce spoke to her. And yet it was a feeling not entirely disagreeable. Nay, perhaps she would not have cared how long she knelt there, listening to the gay banter of that musical voice and stealing sidelong glances through her thick eyelashes at the splendid face which bent over her.

"I shall not let you do that now," said Mr. Scrymgeour, "I will gather them up for you. Ah !" he continued, picking out a perfumed twig from the heap that lay on the carpet, "here is a bit of lemon-scented verbena. My aunt has been sighing for one all this summer; do let me take it home for her, will you?"

"No, not that one, Mr. Scrymgeour," said Aunt Amiel, "It has been gathered too near the top of the tree, and will not grow. Slips should always be taken off as near the root as possible, and cut just above a joint; look, this way," and Mrs. Grey showed him what she meant with a bit of myrtle that lay near her.

It was all the same to Mr. Scrymgeour whether he talked about the intoning of litanies or the propagation of slips. Nothing in the conversational line came amiss to him. With an air of profound interest he turned to Mrs. Grey and received from her a long lesson in the setting of verbena plants. One might have imagined, from the earnestness with which he listened, that he looked forward to obtaining his livelihood as a nursery gardener.

It was Cuthbert Scrymgeour's way to exhibit the semblance of deep interest in any subject that was brought before him. Much of his popularity he doubtless owed to this elastic power of accommodation. People like to feel that they are being listened to and attended to with manifest deference. It pleases their vanity, or if, like Mistress Amiel Grey, they have no vanity, it pleases their benevolence to think that they are imparting instruction and amusement. Cuthbert knew this, and acted accordingly. Like an India-rubber band he expanded and contracted himself to suit all sizes and circumstances.

Some men have a fixed, unalterable purpose in their characters. They are like crown Imperials, shooting up erect, skywards, putting out a leaf now and then by the way, which is fair and pleasant to look upon; but the main life and energy of the plant climbs steadily upwards, until at last it blooms out into one glorious coronal of golden flowers, the pride and splendour of the garden. And some men are like annuals which come to perfection in a week or two, and die when a shower of rain or over much sunshine beats upon them; —trim, dainty, compact little plants, blossoming in the carefully-sheltered flower-beds of society, bristling all over with leaves and buds, ready to put out a flower here and there and everywhere just as may be most convenient, and collapsing at last, when the little bit of root has withered, into a shapeless tissue of dry fibre. Yet, ask any lady florist which she likes best, and the tiny annual is sure to have the preference. The imperial flower, with its crown royal and affluence of vitality, is quite out of her line.

Cuthbert Scrymgeour, B.A., belonged to the "early July annual" tribe of human plants. Like certain vegetable productions in the garden of Eden, he was pleasant to the eye, and also, in a figurative sense, good for food, so long as the tickling of the palate and not the sustentation of life was the end to be answered by partaking. He could be all things to all men. He was quick to discern character, and as quick to adapt himself to it if need be. With a young girl he could discuss songs and fancy-work; with a learned divine the doctrines of predestination and free-will. His fellow-students at Oxford found him *au fait* on the subject of fancy ties; the professors found him equally accessible in Latin roots and equations. He could talk by the half hour to a country squire of hounds and harriers, and then go and gossip with my lady on the beauties of a new Berlin wool pattern. He would quote sonnets—dozens of them—to a sighing nymph who thought herself misunderstood and unappreciated, sympathize with her yearnings and aspirations until she was ready to throw herself into his arms in an ecstacy of gratitude, and before an hour had passed he would be arranging bets with a fast young lady who voted him a "perfect brick of a fellow."

What he proposed this morning was to make himself agreeable to Mistress Amiel Grey, and he did it so effectually that when, after sitting nearly an hour with the old lady, he rose to depart, she was quite loth to let him go, and pressed him kindly to repeat his call.

"Alice," she continued, as he left the room,

"you will take Mr. Scrymgeour into the garden and gather him two or three slips of that lemon-scented verbena, and then, perhaps, he would like to go through the greenhouses; the geraniums and heaths are very fine just now, Frank tells me."

Of course Mr. Scrymgeour would be delighted. He had a perfect passion for flowers, they had been his delight ever since he was a boy; indeed, nothing was such a treat to him as a walk through a garden, especially such a garden as that which surrounded the Old Lodge—together with a great deal more to the same effect.

Alice led the way. Whether the verbena slips were fractious and refused with due filial affection to part from the parent stem, or whether the hothouse, with its endless variety of tints and perfumes, beguiled them into oblivion of time and tide, or whether they loitered to handle and taste the purple clusters of the vinery, or whether Alice lost herself and her companion too in the tangled beech-bound alleys of the Old Lodge garden, this chronicle sayeth not; but certainly a full hour passed after they had bidden farewell to Aunt Amiel, before Mr. Cuthbert Scrymgeour got fairly started home, or Alice found her way back again to the scattered leaves and the oriel room.

David Bruce's music remained *in statu quo* all that day.

CHAPTER VI.

"I SUPPOSE she can line a fellow's pockets nicely, Aunt."

"My dear Cuthbert, I am not acquainted with Miss Grey's capabilities as a sempstress. I have no doubt, however, that in addition to the usual accomplishments imparted to her sex, Mrs. Amiel Grey would devote special attention to the more useful branches of feminine education; and if I were asked to give my opinion, I should say that a due amount of proficiency in needlework, both fancy and plain, is an indispensable requisite in every young lady of birth and breeding."

Mrs. Scrymgeour always talked in paragraphs,

as if her utterances were intended to be set up in type and handed down to posterity by means of the printing press.

Cuthbert Scrymgeour tweaked his whiskers impatiently, and then to atone for his rudeness, stroked them down with his ringed fingers.

"Now Aunt," he said, "what's the use of pretending you don't understand what a fellow means; you can't expect me to clip my words when I'm talking to you, as if the Dean and Chapter were at my elbow. About the young lady's figure, that's what I mean."

"I suppose," continued the Archdeacon's widow in the same precise measured tones, "I suppose you have already had sufficient opportunity of satisfying yourself as regards that matter. Miss Grey, you are aware, is not tall, but she is exceedingly well-made and very graceful in her carriage. I might add that a slight accession of dignity would, in my opinion, be considered an improvement."

Cuthbert flung himself out of his seat and strode up and down the long dining-room of Chapter Court several times before he vouchsafed an answer. At last he drew up abruptly in front of his aunt.

"Take care," she said quietly, "you are treading on my work;" and she gathered away the crimson velvet altar-cloth—it was nearly finished now—from the tip of the Wellington boot which had come into alarming proximity to it.

"Confound your work," answered the amiable Cuthbert, "and you too," he added in a whisper. "I want to know how much money the young lady is likely to have. There now, can you understand that? I believe it is what people call plain English."

"Mrs. Amiel Grey has a very handsome annuity from an assurance effected by the late Dean, which ceases upon her death. What her own private property amounts to, I am not in a position to say. The Old Lodge, together with the estate at Norlands belongs to herself, as also one or two houses in the High Street. Mrs. Grey is reserved in discussing her pecuniary matters, especially in so far as her niece is connected with them, and, therefore, I have not been able to arrive at a perfectly accurate conclusion respecting Alice Grey's prospects. I have every reason to believe, however, and I think I may authorize you in acting according to that supposition, that Miss Grey will be her aunt's sole heiress."

Mrs. Scrymgeour paused to collect her thoughts after this lengthy compository effort. Most authors would have done the same.

"Good gracious, aunt," said Cuthbert, "your sentences are like the streets of St. Olave's, it always takes two people to see from one end to the other of them."

Mrs. Scrymgeour took no notice of this compliment, but went on counting the threads of the monogram she was copying. Under certain circumstances she was not easily provoked. Cuthbert Scrymgeour, B.A., graduate of Magdalen College, Oxford, and nephew of the late Archdeacon Scrymgeour, was the sole remaining prop round which the creepers of her ambition found room to twine. Hereafter she hoped to shine in the beams of his reflected dignity, as she had formerly expanded in those of her late husband. Cuthbert was getting on well in his profession. Already he was ordained to a curacy—not anything very magnificent certainly, but from that she hoped ere long to see him emerge into a vicar-choral at the Cathedral, then he would become a minor canon, next a canon-resident, then a prebend, then an archdeacon: nay, the far-reaching vision of fond ecclesiastical hope overleaped time and distance, and beheld this latest scion of the Scrymgeour family in all the glory of satin cassock and lawn sleeves, dispensing the benediction from beneath the richly-carved and fretted canopy of the Bishop's chair of state.

These ambitious views had recently received new impetus from an idea which had suggested itself to the mind of Mrs. Scrymgeour of bringing about a matrimonial alliance between her nephew and Alice Grey. The late Dean had had considerable political influence. Mistress Amiel Grey herself had connexions in the Government, whose interest might be vastly beneficial in an ecclesiastical point of view; and if the co-operation of these could be secured, Mr. Scrymgeour's speedy preferment was a matter of certainty. She watched, therefore, with quite maternal interest, and facilitated as much as possible her nephew's attentions at the Old Lodge.

Her statement with regard to Miss Grey's pecuniary affairs produced a soothing effect.

Cuthbert subsided into his chair, and meditated blandly on his polished boots. The Scrymgeours had always been remarkable for such exquisite hands and feet, and all the physical excellences of his race appeared to have reached their perfection in the person of this its last representative.

"She's a neat girl," he said, after a pause, "a very neat girl, and, to tell you the truth, Aunt, I have a notion she doesn't dislike me."

"Of course not," replied his aunt; "your personal appearance, together with numerous social advantages which it is needless to specify, altogether preclude the possibility of such a state of mind on the part of any young lady towards whom you think it advisable to manifest a preference; and I am convinced that you have only to be more marked in your attentions towards Miss Grey, who is, as you remark, exceedingly prepossessing, to ensure a favourable result."

Mrs. Scrymgeour paused to take a fresh needleful of gold thread, and then continued—

"Still, however, Cuthbert, I should be guilty of an unpardonable oversight of those principles that have influenced my conduct during the whole of my residence in St. Olave's, and in which I am proud to say I was always supported by your late esteemed uncle, did I neglect to remind you that there are other qualities, apart from the evanescent charms of figure and complexion, that are indispensable to any matrimonial alliance; and without which wealth and beauty would entirely fail to win my cordial acquiescence."

Of course, anyone might have expected that after this promising prologue, Mrs. Scrymgeour would at once launch forth into a neat little exhortation on moral character, purity of thought and life, diligence, courtesy, charity, and other mental qualifications which are usually deemed desirable in the help-meet of one who has the cure of souls committed to him. But Mrs. Scrymgeour did nothing of the sort.

"Descent, my dear Cuthbert," she continued, in the tone of one who is enunciating a weighty axiom, "aristocratic descent, good blood and high-breeding, are indispensable to a clergyman's wife. Without these your position would be nothing, absolutely nothing. Remember, Cuthbert, that the clergy, especially in and about St. Olave's, mix with the highest ranks of society, and it would wound me more than I can express, were I to see you united with one who would not by her own family connexions and unblemished pedigree, fully sustain herself amongst that circle in which your wife will be placed."

"I fancy the little girl is tolerably well connected, isn't she? I always understood the Greys came of a good stock."

"Exactly so; and that is why your views with regard to her meet with my cordial approbation. There is also one other subject that I may mention as investing the proposed alliance with additional eligibility. You are aware that the late Dean Grey had connections in the Government, and Mistress Amiel Grey still retains the interest which he possessed in that direction. You will perceive, without further explanation on my part, to what I refer." And then Mrs. Scrymgeour entered into the ecclesiastical bearings of the subject.

"Hold hard there, Aunt," said Cuthbert, interrupting her in the midst of an elaborate period, and looking out through the tall, narrow window into the sunshiny Close, "who is that splendid woman just going past the Residence, that one, I mean, in the black cloak?"

"If you refer to the tall lady in the silk dress, her name is Edenall."

"Jove, what a majestic creature! Zenobia herself couldn't match that tread—it is perfectly imperial; and what a stately carriage! I didn't think the St. Olave's workshops could turn out such a first-rate article. What is she, aunt?"

"I am not acquainted with her. She brought no introductions when she came to the place, and therefore none of the Close families have called upon her. She lives with the Bruces at Westwood,—lodges with them, in fact. I should not have minded leaving a card, as I fancy from her manners she is a person of family, but such an attention would have involved me with the Bruces, and I have set my face against visiting them until their antecedents are more satisfactorily ascertained. Indiscriminate politeness is my abhorrence."

"I suppose that was the male Bruce I took the shine out of the other night—a shaggy sort of animal that looked as if he might have gone to a dancing-school with the bear in the Zoological Gardens. Miss Grey introduced him to me as if he was quite up to the mark, but I didn't feel exactly disposed to do the polite."

"Of course not. I am very glad, Cuthbert, you have a proper sense of what is due to your position. That is the great drawback to Miss Grey's character. She is so exceedingly kind-hearted, not to use a harsher expression, that she quite loses sight of the respect due to her station. Indeed I believe I am correct in saying that she is on intimate terms with the Westwood people, goes in at all hours of the day, and allows them to feel quite at home with her."

"We must get her cured of that failing. What kind of a specimen is the female Bruce?—stout elderly individual, I presume, with curl-papers and no crinoline, goes in for consistency and sick visiting; that style of thing you know, eh?"

"My dear Cuthbert," said Mrs. Scrymgeour quietly; she was determined to preserve her equanimity this morning at any rate; "I wish I could impress upon you the advisability of adopting a more judicious style of phraseology. It is really not respectful, the manner in which you express yourself, and I am convinced will seriously mar your chances of preferment."

"Gently, gently, Aunt," and Cuthbert balanced himself on the hind-legs of his chair to get a parting glance at Mrs. Edenall, who was disappearing behind the porch of the Residence, "don't be so hard upon a fellow. Staring patterns are all the rage now you know, and there's no harm in clothing one's ideas in plaids and stripes by way of a change. You really mustn't expect me to hold out like a manuscript homily."

"I don't expect you to do anything unreasonable, my dear Cuthbert. I desire your best interests, and I feel assured in my own mind that Mistress Amiel Grey will not approve that style of conversation. Do be more clerical."

"Trust me, Aunt. I can fit the old lady like a glove, and the young one too, bless her sweet little apple-blossom face. And by the way, to come back to the old subject again, suppose you ask her down here some of these days, and get a few people to meet her; something of a crush in a small way, you know. I should like uncommonly to see how she manages at a quadrille party; fancy she isn't quite got up enough for that style of thing—too much in the innocent blue sash and white pinafore line."

"You have expressed my own sentiments, Cuthbert, though not in the language I should have chosen. Miss Grey, I must confess, is at present slightly wanting in tone and that dignity of manner which is so indispensable to the maintenance of a position amongst the Close families. But you are aware that she has not yet been introduced into society, and therefore labours under disadvantages; I have no doubt, when she has gone through a few parties here and at the Deanery and Residence, she will quite drop that school-girl freedom of speech and deportment, and become all that we could desire. I approve your idea, Cuthbert, and will see that it is carried out when a suitable opportunity offers."

"That's right, Aunt, and now I'm off. I promised Madden I would stroll to the barracks with him and see the men on parade this morning. Grace sent a message to know if I would do the prayers for him at the Minster, but one can't be always at it, so I declined."

Mr. Scrymgeour brought his chair down again on all-fours, with a thump that made the archidiaconal cat put herself into a posture of defiance, and then he sauntered away, whistling the first stave of "Rosa Lee."

His aunt looked aggrieved.

"Oh, confound it, I forgot. It was a *lapsus linguæ*, Aunt, you know; I really can't get into the way of whistling psalm tunes. By-the-bye," he said, turning back again, after he had got nearly half-way across the hall, "don't you let it out to Miss Grey that I played the organ at the Cathedral last Friday. Between you and me, Aunt, I made a bit of a hash of it; the bellows man didn't work properly, or something, and the Dean sent up a message for me to stop. Of course, she'll never know who it was if you don't tell her."

His aunt promised, and then Cuthbert Scrymgeour lighted his cigar and strolled down the barrack road.

Don't follow him, courteous reader, with over bitter animadversions, as he goes crushing the red chesnut leaves under his patent-leather boots, his felt hat poised gracefully on the summit of his Hyperion locks, his silken whiskers floating gently to and fro, like plumes of river weed under an ebbing tide. It is the misfortune of story-books that they admit us into the private life of our heroes and heroines, and betray, now and then, the creaking of the machinery which moves this complex social system. Every home cannot, like that of Westwood, bear the light of truth to flash bravely and clearly upon it. All his friends thought the Rev. Cuthbert Scrymgeour a charming young man—a very charming young man. You are expected to endorse that opinion, and it will be a great pity if any little chance expressions which have fallen from his lips during the course of this chapter, should tilt him from the pinnacle of your esteem.

Let us trust human nature whilst we can; when we can trust no longer, let us pity; but, until we are absolutely driven to it, don't let us despise those with whom we have been made to share a common brotherhood.

Cuthbert Scrymgeour is the type of a class which will be found in the Church so long as its pulpits are open to men who enter them for the sake of the social rank and status that holy orders give—a class which lessens not, but rather increases, with that frantic rage for "respectability" which characterizes the present day. So long as shallowness and frivolity, garbed in a silken cassock and white cravat, take rank in the best circles of society, men like Cuthbert

Scrymgeour will be found, marring less by their doctrines than their manner of life, that standard of national character which the Church seeks to teach. Most cathedral cities—for it is in these that social status finds its reverent worshippers—furnish one or more of these *dilettante* divines; men more at home in the drawing-room than the pulpit, the boudoir than the reading-desk. And if this delineation of the amiable Cuthbert's character appears harsh and uncharitable, let it be remembered that he comes here, not as a specimen of his brotherhood—than whom there exists not a nobler class of men—but rather as a type of the excrescences which may grow out from even the most perfectly-organized institutions.

CHAPTER VII.

THE reapers were binding their sheaves, and the heavily-laden corn waggons slowly creeping along over the brown stubble fields, when David Bruce set out from Norlands that seventh of September evening. The grey fogs of November had rotted away the last withered leaf, and early winter frosts crisped all the meadows round St. Olave's, before, wrapped in his plaid and leaning wearily on Janet's shoulder, he was able to pace up and down Westwood lane.

His arm had soon got strong again, much sooner than the doctor expected, but the chill which he had taken in coming home through that drenching rain, settled into a slow fever which lasted many weeks, and had well nigh worn the life out of him. As soon as Janet knew the nature of his illness, she told Mrs Edenall, expecting that she would either leave them at once or go to temporary lodgings in St. Olave's. But to her surprise, Mrs. Edenall preferred remaining at Westwood.

"Let me stay," she said quietly, and with more tenderness in her voice than Janet had ever heard before; "there is nothing for me to be afraid of, and I may be of use to you;" and then she added half shyly, and as if ashamed of the friendly feeling which the words implied—

"You have always been very kind to me, although sometimes I have not treated you well. I should not like to leave you now that you are in trouble."

And, indeed, since the time of that pic-nic, there had come a change over Mrs Edenall. She was no longer so exceedingly cold and careless and haughty. She had lost, except just now and then, that fitful impetuous way, that almost imperious bearing, which, although they never told her so, had often sorely tried the Westwood people. There had come into her face a sort of restful look, which, even though it might be the rest of hopelessness, was better than the icy pride that used to reign there.

So she stayed. For many weeks Janet scarcely left her brother's bedside except for intervals of rest and refreshment. All that was needed she did for him. The doctor said his life depended entirely upon careful nursing, so day by day and night by night she tended him until her face became almost as pale and wan as his.

It was not to be idle that Mrs. Edenall remained at Westwood. Of her own accord she took up the little household duties that Miss Bruce had been accustomed to manage, and laboured through them patiently and unweariedly, with such skill as she could command. And it was easy to see that the work was strange enough to her. Except for thinking of the need which prompted her, it would have been almost amusing to watch this proud creature, with her regal step and empress-like ways, meekly learning of the old Scotch servant how to make herself useful; and with the humility of a little child putting her hand to anything that might help to take the burden of daily care from Janet's mind. Her human love seemed to have in it the element of that other and diviner love, that sees neither meanness nor insignificance in any duty taken up and hallowed by the incense of pure motive with which it is offered.

So little by little these two women came nearer to each other, drawn by that sorrow which in its great bitterness reached only one. The morning greeting became more kind, the nightly farewell, once so formal, tender and faithful. Sometimes, when Janet was utterly overborne with weariness, Mrs. Edenall would sooth her in a quiet motherlike way, unconsciously betraying, by chance look or gesture, the infinite depth of feeling which lay beneath that outward crust of habit. Or she would make her lie down on the sofa, and then murmur in that rich voice of hers, snatches of sweet strengthening poetry, the long-ago speech of those who had suffered and been strong, or perchance the grand calm words of Him who spake as never man spake, until the weary look died off from Janet's face and she fell into peaceful sleep.

In time of happiness people may sunder far and wide, but it cannot be so when death's shadow falls upon the home. Hands that never met before, grope for each other in the dark, and their clasp is strangely comforting. In sorrow we must stand together or we cannot stand at all. Often it is to teach us this, only this, that the Angel comes.

Day by day the household at Westwood grew quieter and quieter. Tibbie no longer crooned through the lilting Scotch ballads with which she had been used to beguile her long spells of scouring and sweeping, but crept stealthily about with unshod feet over the stone floors, and a dree, saddening look on her honest brown face. There was no more any music to wile away the lengthening autumn evenings; for the dust had gathered thickly on the chant books and organ voluntaries which lay heaped up against the piano, and all David's oratorio manuscripts remained untouched on the little corner table where he had laid them that morning when Alice Grey called.

"It is impossible yet to say how the case will end, we must wait patiently," was Dr. Greenwood's reply, as day after day Janet's pale face was lifted to him for one ray of hope or comfort. "The crisis will soon be here; then a few hours will decide it all." And so the time wore on.

It was not until about a week after the conversation recorded in the last chapter, that Alice bethought herself of the promise she had made to David Bruce, and set to work in good earnest upon his music. Once begun, she kept steadily on until it was finished, and then set off to Westwood for a fresh supply.

Of late, hopes brighter and more dazzling than those which belonged to the quiet home of the Bruces, had been crowding her life. Still, beneath them all the old friendship lived on, for Alice was one who, though she might for awhile forget, could not easily forsake those who cared for her. The thought of seeing David Bruce again, and having a long talk with him in that quiet parlour, he sitting in his great arm-chair, she on a cushion at his feet, as her custom was, seemed very pleasant. Ever since that evening, five months ago now, when she had knelt by his side, and felt him speak to her through the might of his grand music, he had been to her what no one else could ever be. When they were together, strength seemed to pass from his soul to hers. It was as if the richness of his nature overflowing, filled her own, and lifted her to a higher standing-place. Alice, perhaps, like most other impulsive people, had a good deal of magnetism in her composition, and a character of great *verve* and power swayed her irresistibly. Had this influence been exercised by a bad man it would have cursed her life; she would have been like those ill-fated creatures of whom we read, whose will is absorbed, and whose whole power of action is controlled by the absolute despotism of some one between whom and themselves a subtle magnetic current is continually passing. Exercised, however, by a noble true man, it became to her a benediction, the one great rest and stay of her life. His influence for the present stood to her in place of that other Eternal Power which is the only sure strength of human souls. And far away down in her heart, past all its little weaknesses and frivolities, and idle girlish fancies, there lay, as a strong foundation on which something worthier might hereafter be raised, a never-wavering faith in the truth and goodness of this friend, this David Bruce who had been so kind to her. So long as this faith lasted, Alice could not sink into utter weakness and inanity.

It was the thought of pleasant meeting and still pleasanter heart to heart talk, that brightened

Alice's face, and brought up the deep quiet light which shone in her eyes as she went tripping along Westwood Lane in the sunshine of that autumn afternoon. Robins chirped merrily in the hedges, those great unclipped bramble hedges whose mis-shapen branches held such purple store of wealth for the little blackberry gatherers from St. Olave's. The golden sunlight came sidling and twinkling through the thinning branches of the chesnut trees, and then its rays played hide-and-seek among the piles of browning leaves that lay on the road. And these same leaves, as Alice danced over them, crackled under her feet with a crisp, merry sound, pleasant enough for one to whom as yet the autumn time brought no dim and worn-out memories.

"Is Mr. Bruce in?" said Alice, as Tibbie opened the door.

"Ou, ay, lassie, an' gin he'll ever gang oot mair till they carry him intill the auld kirk yard yonder, is mair nor I can tell."

Alice's bright face faded, and the roll of music which she held in her hand fell to the ground. Tibbie picked it up with a whispered "Hush, ye mun aye be still the noo."

"Oh, Tibbie, what is the matter? Is Mr. Bruce ill? No one ever told me about it."

"An' wha 'd be like to tell ye when there's naebody in a' the toon cares for him gin he lives or dees? He's just wearin' awa' in the sickness, and lassie ye're the first that's come to speer for him. Come yer ways ben, ye'll no mak' a blatter i' the hoose," and Tibbie, to whom the sight of Alice's face, even in its paleness, was as a beam of sunshine, led the way into the keeping room.

Mrs. Edenall was there, mending some linen which had come home from the wash. Was it a dim, misty notion working up in her mind of penance, as well as the wish to help Janet—penance not only for that lately past coldness and indifference, but for some long-ago and deeper wrong, which made her choose the very employment of all others most distasteful? The room had a dreary look. It was exquisitely neat,—nothing at Westwood was ever otherwise than neat; but there was an eerie stillness about it, a sort of shadow from the darkening wing of death that made Alice's heart beat faster as she crossed the threshold.

She walked straight to Mrs. Edenall, and, stooping down, took her two hands in hers, and looked eagerly into that passionless face, over which at last some faint warmth of human love and sympathy had passed.

"Tell me about Mr. Bruce."

That was all she said. No pause for measured greeting; no time for the pleasant conventions of sociality; no room for anything but that short sharp question. What a different meeting it was from the last that had chanced between the two in that same room.

"Mr. Bruce is very ill, very ill indeed."

"And nobody told me, and I thought he was getting well all the time," sobbed the young girl, hiding her face in the folds of Mrs. Edenall's dress. "But he won't die—tell me, you are quite sure he won't die. Only say that." And Alice trembled from head to foot, trembled so that Mrs. Edenall put her arm over her or she would have fallen to the ground.

Some women—ay, and some young girls too—have the warrior's mail and the hero's heart beneath the flowing robes of their calm, gracious womanliness. They can stand firmly at the cannon mouth of some pending inevitable doom, and wait with a certain grave stillness the fatal ball which parts asunder soul and body, life and hope. No quiver, not even the moving of a muscle or the tremor of an eyelid, has leave to break their girded peace. And, if death comes, is it not an old story that dying is ofttimes easier than living?

But Alice Grey could do none of this. All that was in her of joy or passion, pain or fear, came to the surface, and her whole heart gushed out in that one speech—"Tell me, you are quite sure he wont die."

"God knows, Alice." Mrs. Edenall had soon learned to drop the formal Miss Grey, and take hold of Alice's simple Christian name. "God knows; we don't. We must hope for the best. But he is very ill."

"What is the matter with him?"

"The doctor says it is a slow fever. He tells us no more than that."

Alice shivered.

"You are afraid," said Mrs. Edenall; "some people are very nervous about illness. Tibbie ought not to have asked you to come in. You must not stay."

"I don't think I am afraid, only I'm so sorry. Something aches very much. And what does Miss Bruce do?"

"She is with him always, she never leaves him at all."

"Do you mean she sits by him all day, never anyone else but her?"

"Yes, and all the night, too. Dr. Greenwood says he must have uninterrupted attention."

"Oh, Mrs. Edenall, how tired she must be!"

It was a simple remark, and very natural for one who had not felt as yet that which every woman, be she queen or peasant, must sooner or later learn, the bitter-sweet of love's anxiety. Mrs. Edenall looked through and through that fair young face which held no *remembrance* of sorrow; nothing but the shade of grief which her own words had brought into it.

"Alice," she said, "you don't know what it is to have anyone you love, very ill, so ill that death may come at any time."

Few people have need to pause for thought ere they answer such a question. Most home gardens have given a flower to the great reaper, and he has left in its place a memory which can never die. But Alice's flowers were ungathered yet, and so she answered without pause,

"No. I have nobody but Aunt Amiel, and I don't know that she has ever been ill at all. I have never had anything to do with ill people, nor seen any one die."

"Neither have I, Alice. God never let me comfort any one. Perhaps I have not deserved it. But you will know some day that it can never tire us to do anything for those we love."

Alice sat still for a while, the slow tears dropping one by one to the floor. At last she lifted her face and threw back the long curls which covered it.

"I brought back Mr. Bruce's music, and I must take some more. I know he wants to have it done."

She went to the little table in the corner and began with grave reverent care to turn over the sheets of music which lay in the portfolio.

"When these separate voice parts are done, it will be all ready. I will make haste and finish them. He will be pleased then. He will want to look over them as soon as he gets better, and if—if——"

Here Alice broke down into a passionate fit of crying. The sight of David Bruce's music, his unfinished scores, the pens that he used lying just as he was wont to leave them, brought back the remembrance of him too strongly; and thinking of the pleasant times they had spent together, that little "if" seemed linked to such a fearful possibility of blank disappointment.

Mrs. Edenall came and stood by her, holding her hand firmly and tenderly until the passion of her grief had spent itself. It did not last long.

"There, I shall not let you stay now. You are nervous and overwrought. Walk quietly home, and I think you ought not to come again; it is not safe for you. You will hear as soon—as any change takes place."

Oh! how unwilling we are to frame in our own thoughts, or speak into the unconscious air, that grim word, *Death*. How vainly we strive to shroud it in speech which may not smite the ear with such an icy sound. And even when the sharp glitter of the scythe is blinding our eyes, and there is no longer any hope for the saving of our treasures, still we will not talk of the great, unalterable, fatal Thing which comes so near, but mutter vaguely of a "change."

Alice gathered up the music and went slowly into the garden. Everything looked very different now. If the birds sang in the trees, she did not hear them. There was no beauty for her in the golden sunlight streaking down through the chesnut branches and lying in soft quivering flakes on the grass at her feet. There was no need either, coming home, to break off now and again from a measured walk to a gay tripping dance that should better match the music in her heart. In truth, the knowledge of David Bruce's danger coming so suddenly upon her, had been a great blow. For the first time, when the stay was near being removed, she felt how strongly she had grasped it. Other people might court and flatter her, but somehow for real rest, for strong thorough confidence, she always turned to David Bruce. And whenever she thought of him, spite of his rugged manner and rough stern voice, there would come into her mind the burden of an old song she once read—

> "Douglas, Douglas, tender and true!"

The walk from Westwood was a very dreary one. And then when she got home to the Old Lodge she had to tell Aunt Amiel all about Mr. Bruce's illness, and that brought the sad feeling back again. It was because of these thoughts working up in her mind that there came over Alice's face as she looked away through the clasping ivy of the oriel window into the dim, quiet Close, a softening overtone of pensiveness, a half perceptible haze of sadness, which, like the finishing touches put by artists on too bright pictures, seem to blend the whole into a quieter, more winning beauty.

Mr. Scrymgeour came that night to bid them good-bye. He was going down into the South for a week or two to do duty for a clergyman, whose health had failed. He soon perceived Alice's altered mood, and with ready tact adapted himself to it. Before, he had been piquant and lively, full of jest and anecdote; now he was subdued, quiet and grave. There was an added tenderness in all his ways, a sort of half-concealed sympathy which seemed to hint of some great deep of feeling beneath. No one knew better than Cuthbert Scrymgeour how to assume this beguiling solicitude, nor how to offer those graceful little attentions which to one saddened by trouble or the shadow of it, come so gratefully. Alice's vanity, at least so much as she had, had been flattered by Mr. Scrymgeour's manner towards her during that first drive home from Norlands, it had pleased her to be praised and complimented, smiled upon and caressed. Now, he reached a deeper, subtler feeling. Then, her fancy only was pleased; now, her heart, more tender and susceptible through this new grief, was touched; and quick as she always was to respond to the slightest breath of kindness, Mr. Scrymgeour's tender manner was infinitely restful and refreshing. So that perhaps it would be hard to say whether a certain girlish grief for David Bruce, or a feeling of pleasure and confidence in this new-found affection which that grief had called forth, swayed her heart most strongly.

The weeks wore on. The last laden waggon disappeared from the Norlands corn-fields, and the people taking their walks about St. Olave's no longer encountered troops of Irish labourers, with clouted shoes and bronzed faces, wending home from harvest work. September passed; October came in with its hazy mornings, its soft, dreamy noontides, its red sunsets; and with its later weeks a little sunshine came back to the Westwood home. David Bruce began to improve. At first, he sat up for an hour or two; then, wrapped in shawls and carriage-rugs, he crept across the landing, and got into the west room—the room which had been fitted up for Mrs. Edenall, but which now she scarcely ever occupied. At last, one very bright morning at the end of the month, he astonished them all by coming downstairs and taking possession of his own place at the fireside. True, he looked very worn and weak, and had shrunk into scarce half his former broad bulk; but the getting down at all was a great triumph, and made them feel as if the old times were coming back again.

After Mrs. Grey had heard that he was ill, presents of fruit and flowers often came from the Old Lodge, with kind inquiries and loving messages for Janet. And sometimes, at noon-day, when the sun was bright and warm, Aunt Amiel would send the carriage for David to take a drive; but Alice herself never came for many weeks.

One day, however—it was about a month after he had passed the worst of his illness—she brought back the music which she had taken home to copy. Janet and Mrs. Edenall had gone out; it was the first time they had ever left him alone, but he seemed very quiet and easy; and so, giving Tibbie strict orders that no one was to be admitted during their absence, they left him to his own meditations, and went for a walk down the quiet road that led to Norlands Cottage.

It was Saturday morning. Tibbie had scoured the front passage, and then set the door wide open, as she always did, to facilitate the process of drying. After this, she went into the back kitchen to "sort" the vegetables for dinner, and was giving her whole soul to the paring of some potatoes, when Alice came up the garden walk. The old Scotchwoman was dull of hearing, so she missed the young girl's noiseless tread, and Alice stood for some time in the entry, debating with herself whether or not to ring. Seeing no one about, she crept quietly to the parlour-door and opened it, expecting to find Mrs. Edenall and Janet in the room.

David Bruce was lying on the sofa, his face half

buried in the cushions, so that she could only see its profile. He seemed to be sleeping, and moved not a muscle as she came forward with hushed, careful step, scarce daring to breathe, for fear she should wake him. Surely the dreams that stole under those shut eyelids must have been pleasant, for there was such a look of peacefulness upon his face, such utter contentment and repose; just such an expression as she had met there often and often before, while sitting by his side in this same room, and hearing him rehearse that grand music of his.

Alice stole up to him, and crouched down on a little footstool close by the sofa. After all, it was pleasant to be near him again; it brought back just the old strong restful feel—as if, feeble though he was, his very presence could keep harm away from her. She bent forward and leaned her head upon her hands, gazing earnestly into his face, while a look of tender thoughtfulness came into her own—a look of mingled wonder, and reverence, and affection. It was there still when David opened his eyes and saw her.

He did not start nor seem surprised. Why should it be strange to wake from a dream, through which, like some angel presence, she had passed, and find her really there, so near that he could clasp her hands and look straight into her honest, truthful eyes. He raised himself a little from the cushion, turning his face towards her, and then she saw how wan and worn it was; like the face of a man who stands yet in the valley of the shadow of death, who has not loosed his hold of the hand which could guide him with a few very short steps back again into its darkest place.

Alice was the first to speak. Whatever else Mr. Bruce had lost, he had certainly not lost any of his old quietness. There was still that steady, bolted look about the lips, that peculiar expression of self-containment and reticence.

"I have thought so much about you. I have been so sorry for you." Alice's voice trembled as she said this, and the tears came into her eyes, but she made a brave effort and forced them back again.

He said nothing, only just held out his hand to her; the poor, thin hand, that had scarcely strength to clasp her own. Alice kept it very fast between both of hers, laying down her warm, rosy cheek upon it. She would have done just the same with a little canary bird, if it had chanced to flutter into her bosom.

"And I have wanted so often to see you, but they would not let me come."

Still no answer, but that steady, earnest look, which seemed to hold more than any words could speak.

"I will come now though, and get a long talk with you soon. I have wearied for you very much."

David was pleased, it was one of his own country words Alice had learned from him, and it sounded so pleasantly from her young, girlish voice. He drew her a little nearer to him, and said in just the old way, that Alice remembered so well:—

"I have been sair weary for you too, little Alice."

"Wha's the maister crackin' tull?" said Tibbie, appearing in the doorway with her linsey apron tucked up round her ample waist, and half a yard of paring dangling from the potato in her left hand. "Miss Janet telled me naebody ava was to get speech of him. Ye'd no ha' come ben the day, lassie, gin my auld lugs had been as licht as yer ain wee bit footies."

Tibbie lacked the *suaviter in modo*, but she possessed to a remarkable extent the *fortiter in re*, which, upon occasion, is quite as serviceable. Tramping into the room with her sturdy, stockingless feet, she laid her brown hand upon Alice's arm.

"Ye maun come awa the noo, lassie," she said, and then, without further word or speech, she conducted the young girl out of the room, never relaxing her hold until she had seen her safely *en route* for the garden gate; after which she returned to the back kitchen, and proceeded with the peeling of the potatoes.

A valuable servant, very, was Tibbie Inverarity.

CHAPTER VIII.

MRS. Archdeacon Scrymgeour did not forget her promise touching the party which had been proposed with a view to facilitating the matrimonial speculations of her nephew. Cuthbert was to come home early in December, and the party ought to take place soon after his return. Mrs. Scrymgeour was anxious that it should be the opening event of the St. Olave's season, in order that Alice might have frequent after-opportunities of seeing society. Of course during this, her first introduction to fashionable life, the young girl would naturally be dazzled by the novelty of the scene, and view it rather as a means of enjoyment than a new and serious phase in the curriculum of social education; but on subsequent occasions, Mrs. Scrymgeour took it for granted she would exercise her powers of observation, and study to mould her deportment after the most approved models of the aristocratic circle in which she was intended to move.

This being Alice's *debût*, Mistress Amiel Grey had to be consulted about it. Mrs. Archdeacon Scrymgeour therefore took an early opportunity of calling at the Lodge, and informing the dear, unworldly old lady, of the pressing necessity that existed for her niece's being introduced to the pomps and vanities of polite life, and of the plan which she had devised for meeting that necessity; keeping out of sight, of course, the little personal arrangement that was to follow. It was one grey morning towards the close of November, when she had seen Alice cross the Close to morning prayers at the Cathedral, and was therefore confident of a clear course, that she opened her commission.

Aunt Amiel was sitting by the fire. On a little oaken stand beside her lay a Prayer-book, opened upon the Psalms for the day. She had been reading, and was now thinking over them with a very calm, quiet, contented expression on her face; such a look as those have whose warfare is ended, and whose remaining little span of life is brightened by coming glory. All the tumult and unrest which those grand old poems breathe, had been overpast by her; all the weariness too and sorrow. As she read them now, she gathered up only the praise.

Mrs. Scrymgeour felt that it would scarcely be seemly to break in at once upon Mistress Grey's train of thought with the subject she had in hand. She therefore introduced a few preparatory remarks, "churchy" at first, but gradually relaxing in their tone, until at last they reached a point where the mention of downright mundane topics would not produce too violent a contrast.

"And now, my dear Mrs. Grey," said the Archdeacon's widow, when at last the little bark of conversation had got fairly launched into open waters, "let me mention a subject that has been pressing upon my mind somewhat frequently of late. Our charming little friend"—they had been talking of Alice previously,—"has already completed her eighteenth year, and I am sure you will agree with me in thinking that she ought to be placed in the possession of those advantages to which by birth and position she is entitled."

At the words "birth and position" Mrs. Grey seemed perplexed.

"I had scarcely thought of it," she said, after a long pause, during which Mrs. Scrymgeour supposed she had been mentally discussing the most eligible way in which the *debût* could be accomplished. "I have always endeavoured to preserve Alice from having too exalted views of her own position, and any consideration to which she may be entitled. There are difficulties connected with her that increase as she grows older. They press upon me sometimes, and I almost think——"

"Yes, yes, my dearest Mrs. Grey, I assure you I quite comprehend the circumstances to which you refer. A young orphan girl, connected with one of the most influential Close families, possessed of such great beauty too, and of considerable pecuniary expectations——"

Mrs. Scrymgeour threw out this last clause as a feeler, being well assured that if the expectations were not considerable, Mrs. Grey would speak up at once and say so. Aunt Amiel, however, let it pass without any attempt at contradiction, and the Archdeacon's widow continued,—

"Pecuniary expectations to a considerable amount, always my dear Mrs. Grey render the guardianship of a young lady a serious responsibility, and I sympathize with you, I most sincerely sympathize with you, in the anxieties that your trust involves. But Alice must enter into society sooner or later, and I am sure you will agree with me that her first introduction to it could not be accomplished more favourably than at a select party, quite select, dear Mrs. Grey, which I think of giving in the course of a few weeks, and at which I assure you I shall watch over her interests with a truly maternal solicitude."

Mrs. Grey yielded—how could she do otherwise, to a proposal made so generously, and combining so many advantages? The matter was settled therefore, and in due time a dainty little note, bearing Mrs. Archdeacon Scrymgeour's crest, arrived at the Old Lodge, requesting the pleasure of Miss Grey's company at Chapter Court on the 20th, with the magic word "dancing" introduced in the corner.

To say that Alice did not look forward to the

event with eager fluttering expectancy, would be gifting her with an amount of mental solidity and fortitude to which she had not the slightest claim. What young girl does not anticipate her first party with longings akin to those the little boys and girls of wandering Israel—supposing their gastronomic tastes similar to ours—would cast towards the land that flowed with milk and honey?

Is not her eighteenth birthday welcomed by every school-girl as the magic gate through which she is to pass into the enchanted circle of society, with its balls and parties, its fêtes and flower shows, its dazzling drawing-rooms and elegant suppers, its tulle and tarlatane, jewels, feathers, and wreaths, its successive flirtations, conquests, and engagements, terminating at last in that climax of magnificent display, wherein beneath a canopy of Brussels lace and orange blossom, and with *éclat* greater than that which once surrounded the far-famed triumphs of Scipio, she achieves the sublime destiny of matrimony? I repeat, does not every girl, trained as most girls now are to view marriage as the ultimatum of social politics, long for the time when she shall be permitted to enter the arena and strive for its wreath of victory? Well, Alice had the common frivolities of girlhood, and if her seclusion from indiscriminate companionship had saved her from much of its hollowness, its precocious worldly wisdom, its shallow schemes of flirtation and conquest, still there was that in her which owned affinity with the charms of social life, and made her count the days with scarcely restrained impatience until the twentieth of December should arrive.

But to return to Westwood. After that last visit of Alice Grey's, David grew rapidly better and was soon able to work at his Oratorio with renewed energy.

Indeed there was need for him to do so. The Oratorio was announced for performance in London on the 20th of December, the same evening as Mrs. Scrymgeour's party. The singers had been for some weeks past rehearsing their parts, and Mr. Bruce was to go up to London early in December to superintend the first performance of it in person.

Only once more before leaving Westwood, he and Alice Grey met; and their meeting was on this wise.

It was the day before he went away. She had come partly to call upon Miss Bruce, but more for the sake of putting off the weariness and *ennui* which often came over her now that Mr. Scrymgeour was no longer at hand to amuse her with his pleasant idle talk, or charm her with those pretty compliments of his. Alice found it hard to turn from the nectar of flattery and caresses to the plain food of common life; and perhaps it was this scarcely acknowledged weariness, this tinge of disappointment and emptiness, that made her seem quieter than usual, and brought into her face a wistful look which David had seldom seen there before.

Mrs. Edenall was out, for it was a crisp, bright, sunshiny day, and Janet was somewhere in the upper regions, busy preparing her brother's things for his journey next morning.

David Bruce had not got back all his old energy, and a long day's work at altering one of the choruses in "Jael" had somewhat paled his cheek, and made him glad to rest in the great armchair by the fire. Alice saw that he was weary, and offered to help him by copying out into separate voice parts the music which he had hastily jotted down on a few loose sheets of paper. The work was good for her, it filled her mind and beguiled her thoughts. As she bent patiently over it, the weary look smoothed out of her face, and there came instead, one peaceful, contented. Besides, she was always pleased to do anything for David Bruce.

He watched her from beneath the hand which shaded his eyes. She sat at the music table by the window. The slanting December sunlight coming in through the lattice—there were no vine leaves now to keep it out—stole brightly through and through the golden tendrils of her hair, and flickered upon the rounded outlines of her cheek and throat. Even in her plain, close-fitting winter dress of dark blue wincey, she made a pretty picture; there was something so fresh and flower-like about her.

By-and-by the last sheet was finished, and she brought it to the fire to dry.

"Is there anything else I can do for you, Mr. Bruce?" she said, as she gathered up the loose papers and laid them tidily together.

How humbly Alice always spoke to this man; how docile as a little child she became in his presence. With other people she was wilful, and showed a certain dash of spoiled pettishness sometimes; but with him she was always tender and subdued. It was with very different tones from those she had already learned to use to Mr. Scrymgeour that she asked—

"Is there anything else I can do for you?"

"No thank you, Alice; come and sit down by me now. It will be a long time before we get a talk with each other again."

Alice came and sat on the hassock at David Bruce's feet, resting herself against the arm of his chair. She did not speak, but looked steadily down into the red firelight. By-and-by she leaned her head upon his knee, and began crooning to herself one of the solos from "Jael."

As she sat there, her face half-turned from him, David took up one of her long curls and played with it, twining it round his fingers, then loosing it and watching it fall in a long waving rippling tress to the ground. While he did so, he thought for the first time how like her hair was to Mrs. Edenall's,—the same rich, changeful tint, golden in the sunshine and tawny in the shade, the same playful ripple and soft silky flow. And then he wondered if by the time these locks were grey like Mrs. Edenall's, they would shadow a face so worn as hers.

"No, never, my darling," he murmured, half aloud, as the thought came over him.

Alice lifted her head.

"What did you say? Were you speaking to me?"

"No, I was not speaking to you."

Her head went down again to its old resting-place.

David Bruce was not in a talking mood that afternoon, neither was Alice. They sat there in unbroken silence until the sun crept away behind the grey towers of the Minster, and the firelight began to have its own way in the quiet little room dancing with pleasant fitful flicker over the old-fashioned furniture, and making strange shadows amongst the leaves and flowers of the mirror's oaken frame.

"It is late, I must go home," said Alice at last, making a move to raise herself.

"No, not yet," and David laid his hand upon her shoulder—just a touch, yet it kept her there.

She obeyed every motion of his will as completely as that petulant, imperious organ yonder, at the Cathedral.

"I shall think of you very often, Alice, when I am away. You have been a great help to me."

She looked up to him with a face so bright in its gladness. To be praised by those she cared for was more than meat and drink to Alice Grey. Did he know it was only because he praised her, or did he think that another and deeper feeling made the clear music of her voice as she said—

"It has been my joy to help you. I wish I could have done it over and over again for you."

"Little Alice!"

The words were very low, scarcely more than a whisper; but surely she might have heard the thrill of feeling in them; surely she might have known that tones like those are never used by any man save to the woman he chooses from all others to be his own—his wife. She sat for a little while longer, looking silently into the clear red firelight. Then she moved his hand away from her shoulder.

"There, I must go. Do not stop me again,

Mr. Bruce, please. Aunt Amiel will wonder why I don't go home. And now, good-bye!"

She held out her hand to him in just her own frank, girlish way. He rose, wearily rather, for he was far from strong yet, and held it fast in his, looking down earnestly into her face, as if searching for an unspoken answer to an unspoken question.

Alice returned his gaze for awhile, and then her eyes fell, first to the firelight again, and from that to the ground.

Why did he not tell her that he loved her? Why did he not break away the dusty old conventions, the cobwebs of rank and position, among which she had been bred, and speak out bravely, honestly, as one human being may always speak to another. She stood there in her affluence of hope, and youth, and beauty—he in his poverty and obscurity, bare enough of money and position, rich only in the coin of earnest purpose, a coin, alas! not current in St. Olave's. And David Bruce was very proud. He would have waited patiently and wearied on through years of toil rather than the woman he loved should step down one inch of social caste to place her hand in his.

Yet he hesitated. It was so hard to let her go from him. She looked so humble, so gentle, as she stood before him with downcast eyes and cheeks flushing in the dim light.

His hand was upon the latch of action; one moment more and the fateful question would have been asked and answered—that answer which, spoken in truth, angels hush their song to hear. But just then another hand was upon another latch. The door opened and Janet came in with half a dozen collars whose buttons needed moving the eighth of an inch farther back.

Their hands unclasped. When and where should they clasp again?

Alice smiled a farewell and a greeting both in one, to Miss Bruce, and then slipped away. Presently she was walking down Westwood Lane as cheerfully as though there were no such words in the dictionary as pain and parting.

"Davie, I have got all your things ready for you, except these collars, which have been rather too wide since you were so ill. And do be careful now, not to forget that chest-preserver of yours; you know so much depends on guarding against cold. Your study coat is in the portmanteau too, but don't wear it except just at night when you are by yourself; it is not fit to put on out of doors any more."

"And," continued Janet, getting out her needle and thread and setting to work upon the buttons, "I should like you to wear that black necktie with the violet spots in a general way, it fits you so nicely; and be very particular about your handkerchiefs, will you? You know the London washer-women are so deceitful, and will change them for imitation cambric if you don't mind."

All which directions David listened to very patiently.

Next morning he set off to London.

CHAPTER IX.

IT was the night of Mrs. Scrymgeour's party, and lights began to flicker from the upper windows of certain of the Close houses, whose young lady occupants had received notes of invitation to the spread. It would be stating a profound untruth to say that Alice Grey did not spend more than usual time before her looking-glass that night. The poet's axiom—

> "Beauty when unadorned 's adorned the most,"

quoted so frequently by people who fancy they know all about it, is a fallacy, a complete fallacy, as the experience of daily life abundantly proves. Is it not a fact patent to any one of ordinary powers of observation, a fact about which there lingers not the shadow of a doubt, that the women whom Nature has most richly dowered with personal attractions, are just the women who spend most time in elaborating their toilettes and labouring to produce a pleasing effect? Is it the plain "young person" who sits for an hour before her mirror, adjusting the fall of a ringlet or coaxing a bandeau into its most effective position? Is it the virgin of freckled skin and dumpy figure who can't sleep at nights for thinking what colour her next new ball-dress shall be, and whether she shall wear blue flowers or pink in her stubby hair? No; these and similar anxieties are confined to the acknowledged *belles* of society, who suffer them cheerfully as the income-tax of beauty. Nor would they risk so large a capital of time and trouble in personal adornment, did not the investment yield a profitable dividend in the shape of compliments and pretty speeches.

A beautiful woman is in the right of it to make the most of the talent she holds. It is no light thing to have a form so lovely that every one who looks upon it is unconsciously made happier. She would be scarcely a woman who did not more than simply care for, who did not reverence and cherish a gift, which is as much God-bestowed as the intellect that directs or the eloquence which sways the passions of men.

And, indeed, to look no farther than the mere utilitarian aspect of the matter—we have come back now to the length of time a woman may reasonably spend over dressing herself—it is well to be leisurely and careful in the performance of a duty in which trifling neglect may lead to disastrous results. Take, for instance, your violently well-informed young lady, your feminine compendium of scientific knowledge, who bristles all over with 'ologies, who cannot open her mouth without, not a diamond, but a *fact*, dropping from it. She is invited to a party, and accepts the invitation; not that she cares for balls and suppers, of course, but society has claims upon intelligent people; her presence will check frivolity, her conversation will ensure respect, &c. She is elbow deep in mathematics to the last moment, telegraphs through her toilette, "fixes up" her hair in a trice, jumps into her dress and is walking through a quadrille within half an hour of the time when she was solving a problem in cube root. The evening is not far advanced before a carelessly-adjusted hair-pin begins to sport itself in the back settlements of her *coiffure*. It presses painfully, more painfully —as only hair-pins know how to press when they are badly put in—it becomes positively aggravating; but the arrangements of the party will not admit of her slipping out to set it right, and she is forced to endure the martyrdom in silent patience. She begins to look cross—how can she help it, poor girl, with that vicious pin sticking into her scalp? And people give over asking her to dance. By-and-by a headache ensues; she can't converse, her ideas collapse, her amiability dissolves like jelly on Midsummer-day, her store of information —with which she was to have accomplished so much—is locked up in a box of which she has lost the key. People wonder at her disagreeableness —of course they do not know the misery under which she labours—and, as likely as not, attribute it to intellectual repletion. The gentleman who escorts her in to supper is disgusted with the cross-grained specimen of womanhood he has taken under his protection, and the poor girl goes home at last weary, out of sorts, splenetic, disappointed, and vixenish. All the fault of that misplaced hair-pin.

I don't blame Alice Grey, then, and I hope you will not, that although it was scarcely six o'clock when she went into her room to dress for the party, the Cathedral bells were just on the stroke of half-past seven before Lettice, the good-tempered little waiting-maid, had adjusted the last curl and fastened the white cashmere wrap round her mistress's snowy shoulders. Then Alice fluttered down the oaken staircase into the empty drawing-room, and lighted a chandelier in order that she might take a leisurely survey of herself in the mirror that stood between the windows. The inspection must have been attended with a favourable result, judging from the smile which overspread Alice's face when it was concluded,—a smile not of conceit or vanity, but simple, innocent pleasure at finding herself so fair. You might as well call a forget-me-not vain when it bends to look at its own loveliness in the stream that waters it, or chide the lily for pride because it stoops its regal head over the fountain mirror.

"Don't I look nice, Auntie?" she said, as she came floating into the oriel room where Aunt

Amiel was sitting in her usual place by the fire; "I never felt so pretty before," and then she turned slowly round that the old lady might get a prospect of her on all sides, while Lettice peeping in at the half-opened door, smiled at the pleasant sight.

Was it a presentiment of what that night might bring, that made Mistress Amiel Grey open her arms and fold Alice to her bosom, closely, more closely than the girl ever remembered being folded there before? Would she keep her back as long as she could from that hollow false world in which she would find perhaps a little of floating pleasure, but surely a great deep of disappointment? Would she keep her darling yet a little longer in that peaceful, innocent, unconscious child-life out of which this night would snatch her?

There was a ring at the bell. It was Mrs. Somers, who had called for Alice. Aunt Amiel was too infirm to go into company, and therefore the Dean's lady was to act as Alice's chaperone.

She gave Aunt Amiel a good-night kiss, and with a passing "Thank you Lettice for spending so much time over me," was whirled away to her first round on the great social treadmill.

"Our pet looks quite charming to-night, she is really a sweet little creature," said the Dean's lady, a couple of hours later, as Alice passed them in a quadrille with her partner, Cuthbert Scrymgeour.

And, indeed, she did look very lovely. She wore a full-skirted white dress of India muslin, soft and cloud-like, looped up here and there with clusters of frosted green leaves and pearls. For a head-dress she had that Venetian cordon of pearls, which the jeweller's skill had converted into a very tasteful ornament. It was twisted carelessly round her head and fastened over the left ear in a loose knot, from which the silver tassels drooped and mingled with her brown curls. There was a deeper colour than usual on her cheeks, and a bright glancing light in her eyes. She was thoroughly enjoying the scene so new and strange to her, and, in this respect, she differed from several of the other young ladies, belles of six or eight seasons standing, who had a hacked, worn-out look, and went through the whole affair as if it was a sort of bore.

"Yes, she is a very passable girl," rejoined Mrs. Scrymgeour, "but if I were asked to give my opinion I should say she would be improved by a little more *tone.* She is just a shade too impulsive. You see, my dear Mrs. Somers, dignified manners are so very essential to young ladies, in a Cathedral city especially; and for a person of Miss Grey's position, destined to be the wife of——"

"What, engaged already!" exclaimed the Dean's lady.

"Oh no, no, nothing of the sort," and Mrs. Scrymgeour stooped down to arrange a refractory fold in her black velvet dress, "nothing of the sort; but you see, Mrs. Somers, she is sure to marry into some of the Close families, and she will never get on without dignity. She has quite the air of the nursery about her."

"That is because she has never been to school. It's a thousand pities Mrs. Grey didn't give her two or three years at Madame Bresiatellie's in London, it would have been the making of her. My eldest girl was a terrible hoyden before she went there, but really the change when she came home for the first holidays was marvellous; such exceedingly finished manners, and her tone everything that could be wished."

"Ah, but you see Mrs. Grey has such peculiar notions; it is a perfect mystery to me the way she has brought up that niece of hers. Would you believe it, I had quite a struggle to get Alice to-night, the poor old lady seemed so afraid of letting her be introduced into society. Age, you see, the infirmities of age."

"We were discussing Miss Grey," continued the Archdeacon's widow, as Mrs. Colonel Spurge, a stout dowager of fifty-five, deposited herself on the lounge besides them. "You know this is her *debût*."

"Pretty little thing, very pretty little thing," said Mrs. Spurge, carelessly quizzing Alice through her gold-mounted eye-glass, "but decidedly too *petite* for my fancy. I prefer girls of more build and presence," and the Colonel's lady looked complacently down to the far end of the room, where her daughters, the Misses Spurge, two extensive, good-tempered, unbetrothed damsels, were disporting themselves in the dance.

"Tastes differ. Now I believe most gentlemen are fond of little women. Cuthbert dotes upon a *petite* figure, and you know his taste is universally considered unexceptionable. But Canon Wilkes is coming; excuse me, I must go and introduce him to a few of the gentlemen;" and Mrs. Scrymgeour moved away, leaving the two ladies to finish their conversation.

Generally speaking there was not much interest in the Close parties. St. Olave's was very different to Belgravia, which rejoices in a vast floating population of fresh faces, so that the giver of entertainments can get together every night twenty or thirty distinguished strangers as easily as she orders her supper or bespeaks her decorations. In the circumscribed fellowship of the Close families, everybody knew who everybody else was. The faces which one by one bloomed into young ladyhood, or shot forth the masculine adornment of whiskers, were as familiar as the Close elm trees and the rooks which colonized the Deanery chimneys. The advent of a downright stranger into the select midst of the St. Olave's inner circle created almost as much curiosity as if a fresh gurgoyle had struggled out beneath the Cathedral eaves, or a supernumerary martyr, with palm crown and flowing robes, taken his place amongst the worthies who kept watch upon the east front.

But though the faces of the people were not new

to Alice, their ways were quite strange. Brought up as she had been in the old world stillness of Aunt Amiel's home, even this sombre exhibition of gaiety at Chapter Court appeared a whirl of excitement. The *debût* was quite a success so far as popularity went. The unspoiled freshness of her manner had a charm about it which fascinated the starched cavaliers of the Close. She floated through dance after dance, much to the secret annoyance of certain last year's belles, who were condemned to wallflowerism most of the evening; and it was not until her little feet were completely tired that she came and sat down on a velvet lounge by the side of Miss Fullerton, the daughter of the county member, a fashionable young lady, fresh from town.

"This is your first turn out, I suppose," said Miss Fullerton, as she drew aside half an acre of pink silk flounces to make room for Alice's white draperies.

"Yes. I was never at a real party before. I never saw so much gaiety in all my life."

Miss Fullerton's aquiline nose uplifted itself slightly, and she replied with the air of a young lady who has seen the world—

"Oh this is nothing, positively nothing. It's just like going to sea in a washing-tub. You must get your aunt to let you have a few weeks in town. We think nothing there of dropping into half-a-dozen balls in a night."

"But your shoes," said Alice, looking down at the little white satin tips peeping out from her dress, "I'm sure mine are begining to wear already. I don't think I could dance another set in them."

"Oh," laughed the experienced belle, "you would ruin the shoe shops if you capered away at the rate you have been doing this evening. Three or four quadrilles are as many as any young-lady thinks of going through at one spread, and the rest of the time is spent in flirting, which is much pleasanter. But then, you know, St. Olave's is so awfully slow: one scarcely sees a fresh face — I mean one under a hat — from Christmas to Lent."

"Here's Captain Madden coming this way," said Alice; "he is going to ask you to dance."

"Then he won't get me, that's all. My performances in that line are concluded for to-night. No, he is not coming, though; he has weighed anchor alongside of Miss Spurge. I wonder how it is that small men have such a partiality for high latitudes in women. He looks like a little steam-tug beside a man-of-war in full sail. But here is Mr. Scrymgeour making his way in our direction. What a splendid fellow he is!" And Miss Fullerton began to smooth her bands and manipulate her ivory fan, in anticipation of a flirting opportunity with the B.A.

But Mr. Scrymgeour's errand was not to the London belle; he had business of another kind to be got through with to-night, and a favourable opportunity for transacting it had just offered. He bowed gracefully to Miss Fullerton, and then gave his arm to Alice.

"I believe there is music going on in the small drawing-room, and I know you enjoy singing. May I have the pleasure?" He laid his hand upon hers with a gentle touch, which Alice had felt more than once that evening, and which, every time she felt it, made her little heart flutter with a strange, new tremble of pleasure.

Miss Fullerton shook out her pink flounces, and looked round for a fresh quarry. It presented itself in the shape of Mr. Lewis Thorpe, a rising barrister on the northern circuit; a brilliant young man, with a considerable flow of talk and an aptitude for flirtation, which made him a charming companion to the ladies.

When Alice and Mr. Scrymgeour reached the music-room, Miss Somers was sitting at the piano with Blanche Egerton, a tall, dreamy-eyed, stylish-looking brunette, in lemon-coloured cashmere and black lace, by her side.

"Oh, Mr. Scrymgeour," said the Dean's daughter, "you are the very person we want. We have been trying to get a bass voice for the 'Wreath.' Now, you will sing it, won't you? I know you can do it so splendidly."

"Mr. Scrymgeour's harp is always in tune," said Blanche Egerton, giving him a soft glance from beneath her long black eyelashes, and placing herself so that the Spanish beauty of her complexion should appear in favourable contrast with Alice's blonde face and sunny curls.

As Cuthbert frequently informed his college friends, he "rather liked a dark girl," but he had reasons for preferring the rosebud style of beauty this evening. They arranged themselves at the piano. Miss Somers played, Blanche Egerton stood beside her, and Mr. Scrymgeour a little behind, with Alice at his left hand. She would have slipped away from them, but Cuthbert, unseen by the other two ladies, placed his foot on the hem of her dress, and kept her near him.

Long ago, I heard of a lady who won her husband by the singing of that song. Euterpe and Erato both must have presided with special care over its composition, for its bewitching notes helped to gain Cuthbert Scrymgeour his betrothed. Alice felt rather than saw that his eyes were upon her as he sang those lines, which have doubtless opened the way to many a flirtation, ending in a chaplet even more fragrant than the one they so glowingly describe:—

> "The beauteous wreath that decks her head,
> Forms her description, her description true;
> Hands lily white, lips crimson red,
> And cheeks, and cheeks of rosy hue."

"Now let us have 'Juanita;'" and Mr. Scrymgeour took that song of Spain from a quantity of music which was thrown carelessly on the piano. "Miss Egerton, I am sure, will oblige us."

Miss Egerton smiled; she was quite agreeable.

"Juanita" was her sensation song; it suited both her face and her voice. She dispread her lemon cashmere gracefully over the music-stool, tucked her gloves and handkerchief behind the desk, and was just commencing, in a dulcet contralto voice, to inform her audience that

> "Soft o'er the fountain,
> Lingering falls the southern moon,"

when the door opened.

"Miss Somers and Miss Egerton are wanted for a charade," said Captain Madden, bringing in a list of ladies' names. "Pardon me, Mr. Scrymgeour, for depriving you of two of the graces," continued the gallant little officer, as he gave an arm to each of the ladies and 'squired them away to the great drawing-room.

"He has left me the fairest of the three," murmured Cuthbert in a whisper, which reached only Alice's ears; and then taking the place that Blanche Egerton had just left, he went through her unfinished song in that deep rich voice of his, which, whether it intoned Cathedral services or pattered the airy nothings of drawing-room chit-chat, was full of music passing sweet.

Do the composers of these fashionable ballads ever dream of the mischief which their glowing numbers may work in susceptible hearts? Does it enter their minds that such very demonstrative sentiments put into the lips of musical ladies and gentlemen may slide unconsciously into real feelings, and produce most unlooked-for consequences? Every one knows how that tenderest of tender songs doth end:—

> "Nita, Juanita! let me linger by thy side,
> Nita, Juanita! be my own fair bride."

How, Alice could not tell for certain, but in some form or other she gave the permission so musically pleaded for. Waking out of a dim, confused, and yet pleasant dream, she felt her hand clasped in Mr. Scrymgeour's, and his eyes bent down on her face.

"May I ask Aunt Amiel?" were the first words she could remember, and Alice's answer, whether looked or spoken, gave no denial to the request.

She was yet standing before him silent and trembling, with flushed face and downcast eyes, when voices were heard in the corridor. She darted away through a side door; Cuthbert turned to the piano again, and when a party of ladies and gentlemen came into the room to study their *rôles* for the charade, he was playing a quadrille with the most perfect *insouciance*.

He was claimed to perform Victorian to Miss Egerton's Preciosa in the Spanish Student. He was all polite acquiescence, would do anything in the world to oblige the ladies, and so scarce ten minutes after he had taken Alice's hand in his and murmured over her his pretty words of love, he was on his knees reciting tender speeches to the dreamy-eyed brunette, and rehearsing serenades to be sung beneath her chamber window.

When the charade was over he sought Alice, who had slipped away into a quiet corner of the room, and was sitting in one of the deep recessed window-seats, half hidden by the heavy curtains. There was a flush upon her cheeks and a flickering light in her eyes which deepened as she looked up and saw Cuthbert coming towards her.

"Alice, you look so sweet to-night."

It was the first time he had called her by her name. She looked up shyly into his face, and said in just her innocent way:—

"I am glad you like me. Aunt Amiel said before I came, she had not seen me look so pretty before."

Cuthbert Scrymgeour scarcely knew whether to laugh outright at the child's unbounded simplicity, or to set etiquette at defiance and press a kiss on the lips which had just uttered such a bewitching little piece of *naivetè*. However, his sense of propriety forbid the first, and the second he reserved for a future opportunity. He contented himself with looking into the fair face until it blushed again.

"Miss Grey, Miss Grey; where is Miss Grey? the carriage is waiting;" and the indefatigable captain, who seemed to be the courier-general for evening parties, came up with Alice's mantle on his arm. He was going to assist her in putting it on, but went away somewhat crest-fallen as Mr. Scrymgeour took it from him and signified his intention of acting as Miss Grey's cavalier.

"I suppose the thing is settled," said Mrs. Archdeacon Scrymgeour to herself, as she took leave of the Dean's lady, and watched her nephew assisting Alice into the carriage. "Well, she will make him a pretty wife, and her position is unexceptionable, perfectly unexceptionable. All things considered, the affair is quite satisfactory."

And so ended Alice Grey's first introduction to the fashionable world of St. Olave's.

CHAPTER X.

"TO-MORROW morning I shall come," said Cuthbert Scrymgeour, as he stood by Alice's side in the entrance-hall whilst the footman assisted the Dean's lady and Elene Somers into the carriage, and compressed their turbulent draperies into something like moderate dimensions. And then with a few whispered compliments, which those practised lips of his let fall as easily as cherry-trees shed their blossoms to the May breezes, he shook hands with her, bowed to the other ladies, and the carriage drove away.

Cuthbert did not linger at the hall door to watch it out of sight, as some men would have done under similar circumstances. Mr. Scrymgeour was not one of the subjective class. At all times he preferred action to contemplation, and so as soon as the wheels which bore Alice away began to crunch on the gravel sweep in front of Chapter Court, he went back to the drawing-room and finished the evening by a dance with Blanche Egerton.

When Alice got home, everyone had gone to bed but Lettice, the little waiting-maid. The house had a strange, hushed, deserted feel. The fire in the oriel room was nearly out, only just giving light enough to show deep shadows in the corners of the room, over which, to Alice's excited fancy, weird shapes seemed to be flitting hither and thither. She shuddered, and wrapped her mantle more closely round her as she bent over the flickering embers.

"There's a nice fire in your room, Miss, and Mrs. Grey said you must have some chocolate when you came home, so I've got the water boiling. You're very tired I'm sure," and the kind-hearted little maiden looked sympathizingly into Alice's face, which was already beginning to pale.

"Yes, I'm tired enough, Lettice, but I can't take any chocolate to-night, thank you. Go and make my room ready, please, and I'll come by-and-by."

Never since Alice could remember, had she gone to bed without wishing Aunt Amiel good-night. She could not do so now. As she passed the door of her aunt's room she opened it very softly and went in, shading the lamp with her hand that its glare might not fall upon the sleeper. She parted the curtains and looked lovingly into the old face. Aunt Amiel's sleep was not quiet to-night. She moved restlessly every now and then, as if some painful dream was oppressing her, and Alice bending over her, fancied she heard snatches of broken incoherent sentences.

She pressed a kiss on the old lady's forehead, and then went away. There was a bright cheery fire in her own room. Lettice had drawn up the great easy chair, and put her quilted dressing-gown ready. She was waiting now to take away her mistress's gay dress and ornaments.

"Thank you, Lettice, you need not stay. I don't want anything more. I daresay you are tired too, with sitting up so late. Leave me now."

As soon as Alice was alone, she began to think over all the story of the evening. At first it seemed like a vivid, by-past dream, which indeed might be nothing but a dream. As she sat there in the gleaming firelight, surrounded by the familiar books and pictures, and the quaint black oak furniture, which she remembered ever since she was a child, just the old child feeling came over her again; the fresh, unspoiled, unthinking carelessness of girlhood. Until she chanced to look at the flowers lying in her lap, crushed and broken now, all but one little spray of myrtle which he had slipped into her hand as they stood together in the hall at Chapter Court,—that was green and glossy yet. Taking it up she remembered all, and with the remembrance, there came into her face a look half of wonder, half of womanly dignity; no, scarce dignity, more a gentle, innocent sort of vanity, such vanity as might flush the cheek of a little child who toys with a bright choice plaything.

Two hours ago Miss Fullerton had envied her when Cuthbert Scrymgeour gave her his arm and sauntered with her through those gaily lighted rooms. What would the London belle say when she heard that this same Cuthbert, this winning, fascinating man, the cynosure of half the St. Olave's young ladies, had chosen her, the little girl Alice, to be his wife. Then she recalled his tender looks, his pretty speeches, his pleasant caressing ways. She remembered how proud she had felt to walk by his side all down that long drawing-room, and hear whispered remarks about his noble presence, his aristocratic bearing, his handsome face, and so on.

On the strength of this, Alice began to feel pleased and happy. It was so nice to know that somebody loved her, to feel that she had the power to make somebody happy—for had not Cuthbert whispered in her ear that life would be a blank without her gentle presence to cheer and brighten it?—to feel that she would always have some one now to pet and fondle her, some one who would never cross or scold, but just caress her all the day through. The thought of this filled Alice's heart with new trembling delight. It was very pleasant.

But she never thought of him as one on whom she could stay and trust. Her dreams were of happiness, not of rest.

Alice cared little to speculate on the temporal aspects and possibilities of her new position. Perhaps had the event which now filled her little heart with such store of innocent joy, taken place half-a-dozen seasons later, when she was more cultured by the example of other young ladies, and more experienced in their ways, it might have produced a very different train of meditation. Then possibly that sprig of myrtle might have been not so much a pretty love-token as an earnest of future orange blossom and social dignity. She might have turned it over in her white-gloved fingers, working out, meanwhile, not a pretty vision of kisses and caresses, but a process of mental arithmetic in the rules of interest and fellowship, or profit and loss viewed matrimonially. She might, instead of dreaming over Mr. Scrymgeour's tender looks, have calculated the probable amount of his income; how many servants it would allow her to keep, and whether a pony-carriage or a brougham could be maintained upon it. She might have arranged in her own mind the furniture of her future home, rosewood, mahogany, or maple; also the colour of the drawing-room hangings, and the pattern of the carpet, besides sundry little matters concerning dessert services and table linen, not to mention the wedding breakfast and *trousseau*. For with girls who have been in genteel society for eight or ten years, feeding upon its false maxims and nurtured in its hollow conventions, these considerations are very weighty.

But if the outside shows of her new position found no lodgment in Alice's heart, neither did its infinite seriousness waken any new thrill there. The very unschooled girlishness which sheltered her from the one, made her incapable of appreciating the other. True, she had no brilliant visions of added social position, no ambitious anticipations of married importance and household status, of which that myrtle spray had been the guerdon; but neither did she reck of the treasure she had given, nor of all to which that gift had bound her. She was like a little child playing on the sea-shore, clapping her hands with joy for its curling ripple and the music of its waves, thinking not of the storms that crouch beneath; saying only, as its sunlit spray flashes in her eyes, "O! how pretty!" never "O! how grand!"

The Minster bell had struck two before Alice put off her gay robes, and crept to bed. Soon the room grew dark. The fire burned down until only one single ember remained, which shone like a vengeful eye in the midst of the gloom. Alice could not endure its fixed, unblenching glare, and she covered her face that she might see it no more. But the memory of it would not go away, and the last image which sleep dimmed, was that red, unchanging eye, looking out upon her from the blackness all around.

That same night David Bruce sat by his solitary London fireside, the plaudits of thousands ringing in his ears, his hand still warm with the grasp of peers and nobles who had pressed forward to congratulate him on his brilliant success. Yet it was not the memory of their praise which, as he sat there listening to the small morning hours chiming one by one from the belfry of St. Paul's, brought the grand, quiet light to his face, and the triumph to his eye. It was the thought that now, no longer mean and obscure, but free and equal, a noble man, and a worthy too, he might reach out his hand to Alice Grey and claim her for his own.

Ah, how strangely storms come swooping down upon this ocean over which we drift so blindly and helplessly! Hopes it had taken a life to build up, strike in a moment on the rocks of fate or fortune, and straightway nothing but a wreck remains. *We* would not have it so. Were the winds in our hands, no storm should ever smite the sails, no blast of lightning shiver the tall masts and strip down the pennon which floats so gaily upon the blue sky. All should go calmly, peacefully on, until the vessel anchored—where?

Yes, where? And then we begin to feel the rest, the unutterable rest, of knowing that this whole life of ours, whether we will it so or not, is a plan of God; that the tidal wave of human destiny ebbs and flows in obedience to laws as benign as those that gird the earth's blue waters and fix their bounds. And above all these shifting aims and purposes of ours, these longings and vain outreaching desires, is a voice loving as it is omnipotent, which says to each one of them, "Hitherto shalt thou come and no farther."

CHAPTER XI.

HOW shall I get Aunt Amiel told? was Alice's first thought the morning after the party, when the events of the past night, which had seemed at first confused and dreamlike, began to resolve themselves into sober reality.

Mrs. Grey came down in the middle of the morning. She never rose to breakfast now. This was the first symptom that Alice noticed of her aunt's slowly-increasing weakness. This winter, though scarcely begun, had already been very trying to her. The cold seemed to benumb her completely both in mind and body, and she often was unable to collect her faculties either to converse with others or listen to them. Still, however, she retained the calm placid demeanour, the sweet dignity and courtly bearing that had made Mistress Amiel Grey one of the most distinguished gentlewomen of her day.

"Now, Auntie," said Alice, as the old lady settled herself in the great arm chair by the fire, with "Bogatzky's Treasury"—the usual companion of her morning meditations,—lying open on her knee, "I am not going to let you pore over that old book all day. Shut it up, and I will tell you about the party."

"The party," and Aunt Amiel's eyes had a dim, far-away sort of look. "Ah, yes, tell me. The Dean was so sorry I could not go; you see I had never seen little Dunnie for such a long time, and I was anxious to hear about that poor girl. Dunnie must be quite a middle-aged man now. I always thought he would turn out wild."

Alice looked up into her aunt's face, now for the first time fearing, she scarcely knew what.

"No, Auntie dear; the party at Mrs. Scrymgeour's you know, that I was to go to last night. I want to tell you about it all. Miss Somers was there, and the Canon, and—and Mr. Scrymgeour."

Mrs. Grey paused, as if trying to remember something that was long ago past. By-and-by the vague look faded from her face, and its usual intelligence returned. She was herself again, kind and interested and sympathizing.

"Yes, I know now. I suppose my memory is failing. I get very confused sometimes. Tell me all about it;" and Aunt Amiel made room for Alice to come and sit on the footstool close beside her.

"It was very pleasant," said Alice, as she nestled up to the old lady's side, and laid her head down in her lap. "The people were all very kind to me, and it was just as nice as ever it could be. We danced, and had charades and music."

Alice waited, in hopes that some extempore current of ideas would come to float her over the sandbank of that awkward confession. There was not much time to lose; the morning was wearing on, and ere long the expected visitor would arrive to press his suit.

"It was very nice," she faltered out; "I danced with a great many people, and then I had a long talk with Miss Fullerton, and after that Mr. Scrymgeour took me into the music-room to hear some part songs. By-and-by we were left alone, and then, Aunt Amiel, Mr. Scrymgeour—I could not help it, I don't know what I said——"

Here Alice came to a dead standstill, and her face told the rest of the story. Aunt Amiel put her arms round the young girl, and then rocked gently backwards and forwards in her chair for some time without speaking.

"Already!" she said at last, "I did not think of this. And do you love him, Alice?"

"I—I don't know, Aunt," said Alice, dropping her face lower and lower. "I think I like him very much, and he has been very kind to me."

Just then some one passed the window. Alice knew who it was, and shot away like an arrow, getting safely across the hall before the servant admitted Mr. Scrymgeour. She took refuge in the study, a cosy little room on the west side of the house. This study was set apart for Alice's use. Here she often came to do leather work, or make wax flowers, or dabble in water colours; oftener still to sit in her little low chair by the window and build all manner of pleasant castles in the air, as she looked out into the old-fashioned garden with its boundary of lilac bushes, beyond which rose the crumbling arches of the Monastery. She found her way to that seat now, and folding herself up in the green damask window curtain, tried to catch, through the deep stillness of the house, the tones of Mr. Scrymgeour's voice from the oriel room.

Mistress Amiel Grey received her visitor with a grave demeanour, somewhat more stately perhaps than was her wont, and then waited for him to open his commission, which delicate task he performed with exquisite tact and skill. No ambassador negotiating for the hand of a princess could have done it more adroitly.

"Alice is so young," said Mrs. Grey after a long silence.

"That, my dear madam, is an objection which every day renders less insurmountable." And Mr. Scrymgeour caressed his whiskers, while a dainty, well-bred smile glanced over his handsome countenance. He had assumed a sweetly gentle air during the whole of the interview, as though graciously accepting and making allowance for the inevitable infirmities of declining years.

"She is also very inexperienced," continued Aunt Amiel, "indeed, a mere child in all matters relating to active life. I think as yet she would try your patience very much, she has not even the experience of most girls of eighteen."

"Pray do not let that influence you, my dear Mrs. Grey. I assure you my profound regard for your charming niece disposes me to overlook all possible faults of youth and inexperience. Indeed, the innocent freshness of her mind and heart is in my estimation her greatest charm."

Oh, Mr. Scrymgeour! how could you say such a thing when at that very moment you were speculating on the probable amount of Mrs. Grey's life-assurance, and wondering whether those massive candelabra on the side board were solid silver or only electro-plate.

But Mrs. Grey was not gifted with ability to discern Mr. Scrymgeour's mental processes. She smiled. Alice was very dear to her, and she had all a mother's vanity in hearing the young girl praised.

"Do not distress yourself for one moment, dear Madam," continued Cuthbert, "by supposing that a thought of your niece's youthful inexperience could weigh with me against the truly estimable qualities of her character. Her disposition is so exceedingly loveable that it leaves nothing to be desired in any other direction."

"Thank you, Mr. Scrymgeour. Alice has been a great comfort to me, and I hope she will be the same to anyone who has the charge of her."

After this there was a long pause, during which Cuthbert twirled his watch chain, and Mrs. Grey gazed out of the window, watching the falling snow flakes. There was a perplexed look on her face, a very perplexed look. Sometimes it deepened almost into pain. At last she said—

"There are one or two explanations which I think it right to give, and which are due to anyone who—"

"Certainly, dear Mrs. Grey, certainly," said Mr. Scrymgeour briskly, supposing of course that Mrs. Grey referred to Alice's pecuniary expectations. "I quite understand that."

Aunt Amiel scrutinized him through her spectacles.

"Of course," he continued, "I shall leave the arrangement of Miss Grey's property entirely to your own discretion; believe me, dear Madam,"—and then Cuthbert went through a little piece of self-laudation not needing to be repeated here, in which he put the diameter of the world between himself and any mercenary designs whatever.

"It is not Alice's fortune to which I refer," said Mrs. Grey, "that at my decease will be left in the care of persons appointed for the purpose, and, with the exception of a due marriage-settlement, will be at the disposal of her husband. There are other matters upon which an understanding is desirable. But," and here Mrs. Grey rose from her seat, "pardon me, Mr. Scrymgeour, I find myself confused and somewhat agitated. The suddenness of your proposal has startled me. I was unprepared for it. Let me have time to consider. I will give you a final answer to-morrow morning."

"I am entirely at your service," said Mr. Scrymgeour, with a profound bow. "But, Mrs. Grey, before I go, let me, at least, have this encouragement. Your hesitation does not arise from any doubt as to my perfect good faith and sincerity?"

"Certainly not," and Mrs. Grey held out her hand to him. "As the near relative of one of my oldest friends, I should have perfect confidence in committing Alice to your care."

Mr. Scrymgeour made a second reverence over

the small aristocratic hand which he held in his.

"You will allow me to see Miss Grey before I go, will you not?"

"Certainly, I believe you will find her in the little room on the other side of the hall." Cuthbert Scrymgeour bowed himself out, and so the important interview ended.

The other *tête-a-tête* which took place in the little study did not come to so speedy a termination. There is no need to chronicle the conversation which passed between the parties interested. Suffice it to say that for a full hour Cuthbert's deep-toned voice, mingled with Alice's soft cooing accents, might have been heard in that room if anyone had cared to listen. And when, at last, he took his leave of her, she remained for another hour just as he had left her, her pretty head pressed against the curtains, and a dreamy look coming and going upon her face.

After Mr. Scrymgeour quitted the oriel room, Mistress Amiel Grey leaned back in her chair very wearily.

For a long time she sat there, gazing anxiously out into the Close. She appeared to be striving to solve some difficult problem, or to work her way through some tangled and vexing labyrinth of doubt. Once or twice she looked anxiously towards the door, as if listening for the sound of footsteps in the hall, and murmured to herself, "He should not have seen her; it can do no good, it can do no good."

About half an hour passed in this way. Then she rang the bell.

"Lettice, I want you to bring me that cabinet that stands in the drawing-room window."

Lettice brought it, the quaint, old-fashioned thing that Alice had ransacked the night Janet Bruce came to see them.

"Close to my chair, Lettice; there, that is right. Now my writing portfolio, and the inkstand from the secretary."

"Yes, ma'am, and let me bring you a cushion for your back. I'm sure you look awful tired. We mustn't have Miss Alice going out to no more parties if she makes you lie awake of nights, and seem so weary all day."

"That will do, Lettice," said Aunt Amiel, as the kind-hearted girl brought the cushion and placed a hassock for her feet. But who would not be kind to Aunt Amiel, who would not serve with heart and soul that sweet, gentle, patient old lady who had never been known to speak a cross word to any of her dependants since they came into her service?

When Lettice had gone, she put on her spectacles and opened the cabinet. Everything was in its place, except the cordon of pearls which Alice had worn at Mrs. Scrymgeour's party. There were the curiously-carved balls from China, the fan wrought in delicate lace-work of ivory, the old coins, the pieces of family plate, the jewels and trinkets from India. But Mrs. Grey lingered over none of these. She pressed the secret spring which opened that carved panel, and disclosed the two drawers. Then she took from her watch-chain a tiny key, and opened the upper one. There was nothing in it but the letters which Alice had found, gathered together in a packet, and tied with a piece of faded ribbon. There were seven or eight of them, all written in the same hand and bearing the same crest, an outstretched hand holding a branch of mulberry.

Mrs. Grey read them through, and chose out one. Then she put the rest into the drawer, locked it, and pressed the spring which replaced the panel. After this she closed the cabinet and began to write.

Mistress Amiel Grey had long ago given up general correspondence, and handed over all duties of this kind to Alice. Still, however, her writing retained all its old daintiness and neatness. It was very fine, very compact, quite free from the spidery strokes and fly-away terminals of modern feminine caligraphy. Not a hand of great firmness or decision though, still less of vigour and originality; it rather indicated a character graceful, gentle, orderly.

Writing was slower work with her now than it used to be, and this letter appeared to be one of more than ordinary importance, judging from the frequent pauses she made and the expression of serious, almost painful thought, into which her usually placid features had fixed themselves. She had not written a page when the door opened.

"Luncheon is on the table, ma'am."

"Tell Miss Alice not to wait for me. I shall not come in to-day. And, Masters, if anyone calls, say that I am particularly engaged."

"Yes, ma'am."

During a residence of fifty years in St. Olave's,

Mistress Amiel Grey had not learned to avail herself of its conventional fiction, "not at home." After the servant had gone she wrote on steadily for more than an hour, only resting now and then to collect her thoughts or find words to express them. When the letter was finished, she read it carefully through, enclosed in it the old yellow note she had taken out of the packet, and wrapped them both in two or three sheets of blank paper, which she sealed in several places and addressed thus—

"To my foster child Alice, from Mistress Amiel Grey. To be read after my death."

She placed this letter in the cabinet, murmuring to herself, "If he loves her very much it will make no difference; it cannot make any difference."

This done, she seemed completely worn out. She sunk heavily back on the cushions which Lettice had placed for her, and fell into a profound sleep. The afternoon passed on. By-and-by, Alice stole into the room with a shy frightened glance at her aunt, and then seeing that the old lady slumbered, she crept noiselessly to the oriel window, and amused herself by watching the falling snow. Already it had whitened all the Close, and played strange pranks with the grim old gurgoyles that struggled out beneath the Cathedral eaves, drifting into their contorted jaws and filling the hollow eyes with white balls that glared coldly, stonily down. It covered as with a filmy lace-work the flowing tracery of the great West window; it tipped each leaf and flower of the fretted canopies; it wreathed itself in fantastic draperies round the uplifted cross which stood out against the dim and dreary sky, and folded as if with burial shrouds the saints and apostles who kept their silent watch around the belfry towers. Alice gazed until her eyes grew weary with the purposeless whirl of the falling flakes, and it was a relief when at last Aunt Amiel roused herself.

"Oh, Auntie," she said, "what an immense sleep you have had. I have been here more than an hour and you have not opened your eyes all the time."

"Is it so long, Alice! I did not know. I am very tired," and then she closed her eyes as if composing herself to rest again. Alice did not notice their vacant, groping sort of look.

"Now, Auntie, I really shan't let you go to sleep again. Let me fetch you a cup of tea; that will freshen you up. Miss Bruee says she always gets one when she feels weary."

"No, Alice, not now. Come and sit by me, I want to feel you near me."

She stretched out her hands vaguely, as if feeling for something in the air. Alice brought a low cushion and sat by her, leaning her head upon the old lady's knee.

"You have been a great comfort to me, Alice," said Aunt Amiel, drawing the young girl closer to her. "I shall miss you very much, my darling."

Alice lifted her bright young face to the aged one that bent over her. Could any love of Cuthbert Scrymgeour's be so true as the tender unwearying affection, which ever since she could remember, had beamed upon her from those faithful old eyes, so dim and weary now?

"Oh, Aunt Amiel, I cannot leave you! I will stay with you as long as ever you like. Tell him I can never love anybody like you."

"Alice, my child, my little lost one that came to me so many years ago, why did he leave her?

He should not have sent her away, poor girl."

"Auntie, what are you saying? I do believe you are not wide awake yet."

"I am tired, Alice, and the bells make such a noise. Say they must stop ringing, it was not a proper marriage. He knew it was not a proper marriage. They have no business to ring; they must stop ringing, ringing; stop—stop——"

Alice felt a shiver run through the arm that embraced her. Then it fell heavily down. The tender words died away in a few broken inarticulate murmurs. Aunt Amiel had had a paralytic stroke.

CHAPTER XII.

THE Old Lodge was soon all hurry and confusion. The servants ran hither and thither, scarcely knowing what they did. A messenger was despatched to Dr. Greenwood, and Mrs. Grey was carried upstairs into her own bedroom.

Alice, who had never had any experience of illness, would not believe at first that her aunt's seizure was more than an ordinary fainting-fit, and vainly strove to chafe back warmth and animation to the poor nerveless hands that would never have power to clasp her own any more. Dr. Greenwood came, but did not give them much hope. It was too soon, he said, to pronounce decidedly on the nature of the mischief. He staid long with them, giving them directions about the management of the invalid, and promised to return early in the morning, when he should be able to form a more reliable opinion.

The first thought that entered Alice's mind, in the midst of her confusion and distress, was to send for David Bruce; and the remembrance that he was too far away to give her any help brought with it a feeling of weary, sickening disappointment. Then she would have asked Janet to come; that placid face, those quiet, restful ways, would have made almost any sorrow less hard to bear. But they were very early people at Westwood, and, before any messenger could have time to reach them, the house would most likely be closed for the night. Then, in her extremity, she turned to Miss Luckie, the good, kind, unceremonious little maiden lady, whose heart was as open as her lips, and whose very presence, wherever it came, was as warm and wholesome as a beam of sunshine. Strange that the name of Cuthbert Scrymgeour, as one to whom at such a time as this she might turn for help and comfort, was the last that suggested itself to Alice.

So Miss Luckie was sent for. She made no delay in coming. When Dr. Greenwood arrived, he found her by his patient's bed-side; prompt, calm, self-possessed, ready to receive his instructions and give any help that was needed. Miss Luckie was just a never-failing fountain of tenderness and good-will. Perhaps, on the whole, it was more congenial to the general bent of her nature to rejoice with those that rejoiced; but that never prevented her from being ready to weep with those that wept, and—which is quite as needful—to help them to the extent of her ability. She had had much experience of illness. Most of her own family were already dead, and for years she had tended her mother through successive strokes of paralysis. All this, whilst it had not been able to quench her natural buoyancy of temperament, had made her very valuable at the bed-side of the sick. She had great presence of mind too, never got nervous or excited, still less depressed and out of sorts at the sight of suffering. Added to this, she was swift and nimble as a little bird in all her ways, and there was a certain brisk gentleness about her which, while it soothed, insensibly brightened those with whom she worked.

Alice would fain have remained all night by her aunt's side, but Miss Luckie would not let her. She knew too well that succeeding months, perhaps years, of patient, unceasing ministration would tax all the young girl's perseverance, and she must not overwear herself on the very threshold of her new duties. So at the usual time she sent her away to her own room. It was close to Aunt Amiel's, only divided by a slight wainscotting, so that she was within reach at a moment's notice, if her presence should be needed.

Alice went without a word of opposition. She was docile as a child now, and did whatever they told her with a mild, unquestioning obedience which was very touching to behold. Indeed, she seemed stunned and bewildered by the blow that had fallen so suddenly upon them. It had swept away both will and resolution. She was one of those who in sorrow cling helplessly to any, even the frailest support, instead of being roused by it to intense, active exertion.

She shivered as she entered the lonely room. In the excitement and hurry of that evening, Lettice had forgotten to light the fire as usual, or draw the curtains; and the moonbeams streaked whitely in through the mullioned window, and flitted, like ghosts, upon the black oak-panelled walls. Alice crept into bed, leaving the lamp still burning on the table, for she was afraid of being alone in the dark. Alone in the dark! Poor child! she was only just beginning to grope in the outer shadow of that darkness that comes so surely to us all, and in which, unless God be with us, we can never be anything else but alone.

She heard the Cathedral clock strike ten, then eleven, then twelve, as she lay awake, listening nervously for every passing footfall, and magnifying into terrible meaning every chance sound which broke the stillness of the house. Over and over again she woke out of troubled sleep with a stifling, undefined sense of something wrong, something very dreadful that had happened; and then back again, in all its startling vividness, came the picture of Aunt Amiel lying in the next room, stiff, motionless, unconscious. And in gay contrast to this, as if to mock her with its glare and gaiety, flashed over her memory the remembrance of the night before, its dance, and music, and song; the soft, burning words of love to which she had listened, the clasp of Cuthbert Scrymgeour's hand, scarce cold upon her own. Then, weary and bewildered, she would drop into another short, unquiet slumber, only to wake again with the same haunting fear as before.

The night wore itself away; morning came at last, and, with the first dawn of its grey light, Alice dressed and went softly to her aunt's room. It was with almost a sickening dread that she opened the door. What if the Angel of Death should have come and borne away the poor silent sleeper,—what if that tender benignant old face should already have stiffened down into the rigid marble pallor which no kiss of hers could ever warm or loosen? Her hands trembled so that she could scarcely lift the latch, and her whole frame shook with a vague, shapeless fear.

But she need not have been so afraid. There was nothing in the aspect of the room to remind any-one of sickness or death. A bright fire was burning cheerily in the wide fire-place, dancing at its own reflection in the polished wainscotting. Miss Luckie sat by it with her knitting work, just as neat and compact as ever, her white satin cap ribbons shining in the warm light, her bright little face as fresh as if she were beginning and not ending, a ten hours' vigil of silence and solitude. The curtains of the bed were closed; Alice scarcely breathed as she drew them back and gazed eagerly upon the unconscious sleeper.

Aunt Amiel lay quite still, as if in pleasant slumber. There was no expression of pain upon her face, the mouth kept its old peaceful smile, not a wrinkle marred the smoothness of the forehead beneath its bands of shining silvery hair. She looked as if she might wake at any moment, just her own dear self again.

Whilst Alice was bending over her, she opened her eyes. Ah! something was wanting there. It was the calm, unthinking, vacant gaze of a new-born infant, who looks but sees nothing. As her glance wandered slowly round the room, it fixed on Alice, and then a very, very faint gleam of recognition seemed to pass across her face, and she tried to speak, but it was only an inarticulate murmur. Alice bent over her and kissed her many times, but the eyelids closed again, and that changeless calm came back to the pale face.

Dr. Greenwood returned very early in the

morning. Aunt Amiel lay just as he had left her the night before.

"Mrs. Grey has had a very quiet night," said Miss Luckie.

"Ah!" and the doctor looked grave; "no restlessness at all?"

"No, not the slightest. She has lain quite still, just as you see her now, ever since she was brought up."

"And has no pain?"

"We think not; her face has scarcely moved a muscle."

Dr. Greenwood shook his head. "I had rather," said he, "that she had been more restless." And then in a grave professional sort of way he began to examine his patient.

He staid a long time; then told them faithfully the best and worst of the case The whole of Mrs. Grey's left side was paralysed; the right partially so. She would never be able to speak again, or to move about from place to place, except as she was carried. And with this suspension of physical powers, there seemed to have fallen upon her mind a profound sleep, which neither grief nor pain could disturb, and which would never pass away until the grand and final change. She might live for years in this state, suffering nothing, enjoying nothing, cut off from all communication with the outer world; just eating, breathing, sleeping,—and no more.

Alice listened quietly whilst Dr. Greenwood told her all this. She bore it better than they expected. The one great overpowering dread was passed; Aunt Amiel would not die. Anything else seemed easy to be endured, if only she could look upon the dear remembered face, and fondle in her own the passive helpless hands. She would not be alone, and to be alone was the very thing which of all others, Alice most dreaded. Life could not be quite dark, nay, it could never be aught but quiet and almost happy, so long as no churchyard grass covered Aunt Amiel's head, and no gravestone bore her name upon its marble front.

It is well for us that we cannot at once apprehend the full bitterness and sting of any sorrow which God in His infinite mercy suffers to come upon us. Just so much of it as we can understand we take and suffer, sometimes patiently, sometimes with tears and sharp unavailing murmurs. But not until months and it may be years have passed, can we look back and see how dark has been the road over which our weary steps have journeyed. Alice's first gush of sadness was over, and she thought the bitterness of death was past. It was well for her she did not know that her feet were but just passing the boundary line that divided her young unthinking girlhood from the great wide untried track of life, with all its possible shadows and unrest.

CHAPTER XIII.

THE news of Mistress Amiel Grey's illness soon spread amongst the Close families. The doctor's carriage seldom stopped at one of the tall old-fashioned houses without all the rest speedily becoming acquainted with the why and wherefore of such a proceeding. The Dean's lady was first to hear of the event, and she at once sent a message across to Chapter Court, which reached the Archdeacon's widow just as that lady and her nephew were sitting down to breakfast.

Cuthbert's heart was very shallow, but it was not hard. His first impulse was to set off at once to the Old Lodge and offer Alice such consolation as lay within his reach. But Mrs. Scrymgeour objected.

"My dear Cuthbert, I beg you will do no such thing. In cases of this kind a family is always besieged by inquirers whose well-meant but ill-timed attentions are anything but acceptable. Any sympathy which you may have it in your power to offer to Miss Grey will be more suitable when the first excitement of her aunt's illness has passed over. I will send the servant across with cards and condolences the first thing, and nothing further is needful to-day."

Thus Mrs Scrymgeour, with cast-iron accents and a decisive wave of her hand. Cuthbert allowed himself to be convinced, and the two sat down to a sumptuously appointed breakfast table, whilst Alice was keeping her watch beside the bed of Aunt Amiel.

The dining room at Chapter Court never looked remarkably cozy, and this morning it seemed less so than usual. The snow that had been falling steadily all night, lay in heavy drifts upon the frames and deep cornices of the windows. The sky was grey and leaden, and behind the white undulating pall which overspread the Close, trodden yet by scarce a solitary footstep, the Minster reared its huge irregular bulk, looking terribly grim and swarthy. There was no sunlight to play through the heavy crimson curtains, or glance upon the carved oak panelling, or lighten up the stiff old family portraits which were marshalled in solemn rank and file down the long narrow room; all looked grey and cold and irregular. Even the Archidiaconal cat seemed to have a vague perception of the prevailing uncomfortableness of things, and from time to time, turned towards her mistress with a ludicrously disgusted expression of face. Mrs. Scrymgeour was attired to match the morning, in a severely strong-minded dressing gown of brown serge, unsustained by crinoline, and her grey curls, very frizzly from having just been released from their papers, bristled fiercely on each side of her spare colourless cheeks.

"Poor little Alice!" said Cuthbert, helping himself to another egg. "She'll be terribly cut up about this affair. I believe she thought all the world about that old aunt of hers."

"I have no doubt that the event will ultimately be of considerable benefit to Miss Grey," replied the Archdeacon's widow, in her usual measured tones, a little stiffer perhaps by reason of the state of the atmosphere, "but don't distress yourself, Cuthbert. I assure you I have fully met the requirements of the occasion. The parlour-maid has gone across this moment with cards."

If one of her dearest friends had suddenly been plunged into the depths of adversity, Mrs. Scrymgeour would have forwarded cards and condolences, and on no account thought of offering the balm of personal sympathy until the stipulated period for a morning call.

"If I were asked to give my opinion," she continued, quietly stirring her coffee, "I should say that Mrs. Grey has always been foolishly indulgent in the personal management of her niece, and the event which we are called upon to deplore, though exceedingly painful, will, I am convinced, issue in the material improvement of Alice's character."

"She's such a child too, poor little thing," said Cuthbert, in a softened tone; the thought of Alice bathed in tears, as he had no doubt she would be, touched his heart. "I wonder how she bears it."

"I think I have told you before, Cuthbert," and Mrs. Scrymgeour paused to button the sleeves of her dressing-gown, "I think I have hinted to you before that Alice's great defect is want of self-reliance. She has been thought for, and cared for, and petted, until her character has become quite deteriorated; but I anticipate that her general deportment will be greatly improved by this dispensation."

Cuthbert thought that her deportment would do very well as it was, but he went on buttering his eggs in silence. The event had not affected his appetite materially.

"Understand me, Cuthbert, I feel the profoundest sympathy for Alice, and I intend to avail myself of the earliest suitable opportunity of expressing my entire commiseration with her in the calamity which has befallen her respected aunt. But," and here the strings of Mrs. Scrymgeour's voice relaxed and took on a decidedly buoyant tone, "how exceedingly fortunate, my dear Cuthbert, that you called upon the old lady yesterday and got a favourable reply. I suppose the matter may now be considered definitely arranged."

"I don't know, aunt; it doesn't answer to count one's chickens before they're hatched."

Mrs. Scrymgeour winced. She had a deep-rooted aversion to proverbial expressions; she considered them essentially vulgar. But the solecism was allowed to pass unrebuked.

"The old lady didn't give me a decided answer," continued Cuthbert. "She wanted a day or two to consider before coming up to the scratch."

"Of course her hesitation did not arise from the faintest possible doubt as to your eligibility?"

"Oh, no," and the B.A. stroked his whiskers complacently; "she allowed, of course, that I was quite up to the mark; in fact, the last words she said to me were about having perfect confidence in committing the young lady, &c., &c.—that style of thing, you know, Aunt."

"And I think I understood you that she mentioned money matters in a way that was perfectly satisfactory."

"All right. Whole of the property to come to Alice, with suitable settlements. A nice little penny too; why that oak furniture is worth a mint of money, and the estate at Norlands, if it's unencumbered——"

"Of course it is, Cuthbert; Mrs. Grey's property is entirely in her own hands."

"Would make a man independent. Blanche

Egerton's fortune is a mere pepper-corn to it."

"Miss Egerton has expectations from her grandfather, Cuthbert, which, if reports are correct, are very considerable. But the old man might marry, and then of course she would have nothing but her mother's marriage settlement, which is trifling, not more than a couple of hundreds a year, and that is not worth your attention."

"I rather like a dark girl, though," said Cuthbert, balancing the silver spoon on his forefinger.

Mrs. Scrymgeour ignored this little piece of confidence on the part of the nephew, and continued, in a business like matter-of-fact sort of way—

"Ample means are indispensable for a clergyman. I should be dreadfully annoyed, Cuthbert, were I to see you hampered with a wife who would not be able to advance your interests in a pecuniary point of view. I consider it the duty of every young man to exercise a proper amount of discretion in selecting both birth and fortune, especially a young man in the Church. Indeed, if I were asked to give my opinion, I should say that I am perfectly disgusted with the blindness evinced by multitudes of young men of the present day, who surrender themselves to a pretty face or an agreeable temper or a pleasing disposition, as if these merely natural external qualifications could assist in housekeeping or sustain a position. Your uncle, Cuthbert, the late Archdeacon, was entirely superior to these paltry, and as I may add, perfectly immaterial, qualities."

Mrs. Scrymgeour need scarcely have troubled herself to make this last statement. Any one who looked at the Archdeacon's widow as she sat at the fore-front of the breakfast-table, in her brown serge dressing-gown and rampant grey curls, would have arrived unaided at the conclusion that the "immaterial qualities" of good temper, pleasant disposition, and personal attraction, had not swayed the discreet Dr. Scrymgeour in his choice of a partner for life.

"I am astonished, Cuthbert," she continued, "I am dismayed at the moral obliquity which leads young men of birth and family to bestow the honour of their heart and hand so indiscriminately. It violates all my feelings of—were you speaking to me?"

"A little more sugar, Aunt, if you please."

It is doubtful whether, in preferring this request,

Cuthbert had reference to the expressed juice of a certain West Indian vegetable, or whether he suggested the increased cultivation of that saccharine portion of human nature which, in his aunt's development, was not, to say the least of it, redundant. Mrs. Scrymgeour, however, understood that he wished for another lump of sugar in his coffee, and therefore supplied him with one. She then returned to the subject in hand.

"Therefore, as there was an understanding between you on both these subjects, I infer that Mrs. Grey's hesitation arose from the natural indecision of her character. You are aware, Cuthbert, that she is not a woman of great strength of mind; and a proposal so advantageous in every respect to the position and happiness of her niece, would naturally disturb the equilibrium of her thoughts, and cause her to request time for reflection."

"Fact, Aunt; you're about right. Indeed, she seemed quite come down upon when I mentioned it to her."

"Of course, it was perfectly natural; and, on the whole, I respect her for not appearing too anxious to get her niece comfortably settled. It annoys me to see those who have the care of young people so unwarrantably eager to get them off their hands. Mrs. Colonel Spurge, now, has really done everything with those daughters of hers, but put them up to auction; and Mrs. Crumpet too, though I have the greatest respect for her; still, if I were asked to give my opinion, I should feel it my duty to say that she brings her daughter forward in a manner that is not in accordance with my views. You will go across to the Old Lodge to-day, I suppose?"

"Well, Aunt, yes," replied Cuthbert, whose affection seemed to have cooled down during the course of the conversation, until it reached the Archidiaconal level. "Of course; she'll expect me to turn up before long, only I hope I shan't be expected to pay a pastoral visit to the old lady. That sort of thing isn't in my line, it really isn't."

"Of course, Cuthbert, if you are requested to do so, the least that can be expected from you as a clergyman, is that you should address a few remarks to her."

"But I'm so confoundedly stupid at doing the proper thing to sick people. If one could just get off now with a piece or two out of the Burial Service."

"Cuthbert! Cuthbert!" cried the Archdeaconess, in a state of agitation, "what are you saying—the Burial Service to a sick person?"

"Oh, I say the Burial Service?—well, if I did, I meant the Visitation for the Sick, which comes to pretty much the same thing; but you know it's such a bore having to sympathize and all that sort of thing, when really you don't know a fraction about it. And then ill people always think they must begin and go through the whole story, and you're forced to sit still and listen."

"That will not be the case at the Old Lodge," said Mrs. Scrymgeour. "Mrs. Grey has, if I understand correctly, lost the power of speech, and is unable even to reply to anything that is said to her."

"Ah, indeed," and Mr. Scrymgeour seemed a little bit touched; "well, in that case, it's no use my saying anything at all. But here comes the postman. Good-bye, Aunt, I'm off now. I expect to be back to dinner; but if I don't come, you needn't wait for me."

He called at the Old Lodge in the afternoon of that day. The servant showed him into the oriel room, which remained just as he had left it the morning before. There was even yet a little damp place on the carpet where the snow had melted from his boots whilst he sat talking to Aunt Amiel. Her great easy chair was in its usual place, the loose cushion at the back still retaining the impression her head had made while it lay there in that last, heavy, forewarning slumber. Her oaken cabinet stood by the chair with all her writing materials upon it undisturbed, the blotting-paper bearing the reversed print of that superscription to Alice, and the pen as it had been laid with the ink yet wet in it upon the silver standish. There were a few grey, burnt-out ashes in the grate, and the room had an unkept, comfortless sort of look.

These things, speaking as they did to Cuthbert of the great grief which had fallen upon that house, brought over him a strange hush and solemnity. He seemed to be standing within the shadow of death, and no one standing there can be other than thoughtful.

Alice came to him. The first violence of her grief had passed away and she looked quite calm, but there was still a quiver in her voice as if the tears lay very near, and a single word might bring them gushing down. As she glanced at the empty chair standing by the fireplace, she shuddered.

"Do not let us stay here, Mr. Scrymgeour. I will take you into the study."

He followed her into the pleasant little room on the other side of the hall. Here, everything looked warm and comfortable and homelike. Its belongings did not speak to him so painfully of death and danger. By degrees the awe which had come over him wore off. Still he felt ill at ease. He did not know what to say. He wished Alice would burst into tears, that he might kiss them away, and begin to pet and fondle her as it seemed most natural to do. But she sat in her low chair by the fire looking so hushed and calm, her head bent down, her eyelids drooping until their long lashes almost touched her cheek He thought she would have thrown herself into his arms, and wept away her grief there. Perhaps, had he come to her in its first bitterness, she might have done so, and then their hearts would have drawn more closely together; but all that was passed now.

How strangely any great trouble seems to part our friends from us. In joy and gladness they were our equals, we could walk side by side with them; but when the angel of sorrow stretches out his hand, it is to lift them where we cannot reach. Henceforth they walk above us in a world whose air is too pure for us to breathe.

This, or something like this, Cuthbert Scrymgeour felt as he watched Alice sitting there by the firelight. Such a distance in one little day seemed to have come between them. She was the first to speak.

"You have heard of our great grief, then."

Her voice was very low, but Cuthbert thought it had never sounded so sweet before. He could find no way to answer her. The commonplace words of comfort which he had framed, died upon his lips; they seemed too utterly vain and idle. All that he could do was to draw his chair a little nearer to her, and take her hand in his.

She let him take it, but it lay moveless in his grasp, not nestling lovingly down as if glad to be there. She went on with a sad quiet sort of self-possession:—

"We think Aunt Amiel doesn't suffer much. She lies quite still, but she can't speak to us at all, and I don't think she understands anything we say to her. Dr. Greenwood says it will never be different until she dies. It is so sad."

Cuthbert vainly strove to think of something that would do to say to her, but nothing came. If she had been gay he could have laughed with her, if petulant he could have humoured her, if sentimental he could have quoted poetry by the half-hour; but in this great sorrow which had come down upon her, he was dumb.

He put his arm round her at last, and said tenderly,—"Poor little Alice, poor little Alice!"

She looked up in his face. It was kind and gentle, for indeed he was very sorry for her. Something in its expression seemed to unlock her heart, for she laid her head down upon the hand that held hers, and presently he felt the hot tears dropping one by one upon his fingers.

"You will let me come and see you very often, will you not?" he said, in that luring musical voice of his.

She only answered by pressing her face closer to him and laying her other hand in his. Just then Dr. Greenwood's carriage drove to the door, and Alice started up to meet him. Cuthbert held her in his arms for a moment or two and kissed her very tenderly. Then he left her, and when he got out into the Close once more, and tramped the snow under his feet, he felt like a man who has got through a somewhat troublesome ordeal, and, all things considered, acquitted himself as well as could be expected.

CHAPTER XIV.

IT is strange how soon the sharp edge of any grief wears off, any grief at least which is sent from God, and not brought on by our own blind self-will and obstinacy.

Household trials that seemed at first so very bitter and unendurable, by degrees sink quietly into the current of daily home life, and at last make scarce a ripple on its still waters. By-and-by Aunt Amiel's room became a bright spot in the house. Alice learned to look without tears, nay with a certain thankfulness at the poor patient face, with its never-changing smile of unconscious peace. The tumult passed away, the alarm, the suspense, and things came back again to their former quiet track. Only a few necessary changes were made in the establishment at the Old Lodge. A trusty servant was sent to take charge of Norlands, and Mrs. Cromarty came to the Lodge to attend upon Mistress Amiel Grey. She was a large, strongly-built, powerful woman, able to lift the invalid in and out of bed, and wheel her from room to room in her large couch chair.

Miss Luckie never returned to her maiden nest in the Low Gardens. Day after day Alice begged her to stay "just a little longer." Even after the home sunshine had come back, and that which the estimable little lady supplied was no longer needful, Alice seemed to require some sort of stay and protection. No change except for death was likely to take place in Mistress Amiel Grey, and she had no near connections who could come and occupy her position in the Old Lodge. So after some consideration it was arranged that Miss Luckie should take up her permanent residence there, partly to overlook the general management of the house, and partly to be a companion and protector for Alice.

On the same floor as Aunt Amiel's bed-room,

was a pleasant little apartment looking towards the south. It had a wide lattice casement, round which vines and ivy climbed; indeed there was scarce a window in all the Lodge which was not thus adorned. This little room was fitted up for Mrs. Grey. Alice had it re-painted and hung with choice pictures—not that the poor invalid could derive any gratification from them, but it cheered her own loving heart to feel that even in their unconscious gaze, those eyes should only rest on things lovely and pleasant. Here Mrs. Grey was brought morning by morning, and here Alice began to pass the chief part of her time, gathering round her the little belongings of her daily life, and learning patiently to calm her young spirit down to its new, untried track.

Any one going into the Old Lodge three weeks after that first terrible night, would scarcely have known that a shadow had so recently passed over it. When once the astonishment and perplexity had worn away, it seemed no longer painful even to watch Aunt Amiel; for, waking and sleeping, the same deep, unbroken peace ever brooded upon her face. He who had caused to come down upon her that strange soul slumber, mercifully ordered that no thought of pain or weariness should ever find leave to mar it.

People tell us that in death the last image which fell upon the eye is retained, and that could we lift the unconscious lids the picture would be there. So in this living death of Mistress Amiel Grey, it seemed as if the last impression left upon the mind had lingered there, and graven its memorial in the still face that changed not from that look of calm, benignant, trustful love which met Alice's upturned gaze just before the stroke came that so completely severed her aunt from all human sympathy or intercourse. Was it so that this human intercourse being sealed up, that other door was opened which bars Heaven from mortal sight, and so the soul lived Godwards only, and never earthwards, having no more any voice, or look, or gesture, that human skill might interpret?

And thus Alice Grey's life, though somewhat clouded from its first sunny freshness, was yet full of a certain quiet happiness. Or even, had her home been less peaceable, what life can be anything but happy so long as it is sunned by the promise of human love, and so long as that love is steadily trusted?

Alice's engagement with Mr. Scrymgeour was accepted as a matter of course. Aunt Amiel's last expression respecting it had been one of approval and acquiescence. None had any right to step in between them now. The slight hesitation which she had manifested on the morning of their interview, had passed away from Cuthbert's mind. Alice had beauty, family, and fortune, these were quite enough for him; and Mistress Amiel Grey's present mental incapacity secured him from the loss of the prize.

As for Alice, she was a warm-hearted affectionate little creature. She gave him all she had to give.

It was just her happiness to be petted and caressed, and made much of; all this Cuthbert did, and she asked nothing else. Then she was very proud of him. He was so handsome, so noble; he looked so nice as he stood up in the crimson-lined reading-desk of the Cathedral, chanting out in that grand, deep voice of his, the church prayers: his white robes flowing round him, the light from the stained windows tipping and goldening his glossy hair. And it made the little thing feel quite important to think that he, this handsome, accomplished, fascinating Cuthbert Scrymgeour, this hero for whom half the Close young ladies had sighed their hearts away, should have turned from them all and chosen her, the little girl Alice, to be his wife.

And to tell the truth, Cuthbert was really very fond of her. Her pure, unschooled, innocent ways could not but be very refreshing to one so steeped in the shows and frivolities of fashionable life. He loved her as much as he could love anything. It pleased him to be looked up to, admired, and wondered at. He liked to display to her his knowledge of life, his talents—what he had of them—his accomplishments, noting the while her smile of innocent surprise. It made him feel very big and very important; and how many men in a thousand are there to whom the consciousness of their own superiority is not a balm most sweet and precious? Besides, she was something to play with, one of those gentle, fondling little creatures, who just seem made to be kissed and flattered and caressed, and then, when they grow old—but who ever thought of bright-haired Alice Grey growing old?

But for the exercise which Aunt Amiel's perfectly dependent state gave to the higher, nobler part of Alice's nature, she might have grown vain and frivolous. She was very much the creature of circumstances—just what others made her. David Bruce's influence was withdrawn now; his skilful touch no longer woke from the chords of her heart the music which had promised to be so sweet. There was no one to make her feel as he had done, how little she was, how noble she might be. Only in Aunt Amiel's presence her soul found room to grow. The slight, and sometimes almost unconscious shadow, which that living death cast upon the house, kept Alice Grey from a death more mournful still, even the death of all noble and heavenward thought.

Soon after Miss Luckie was located at the Old Lodge, and things had once more got into a smooth track under her brisk, active management, Dr. Greenwood sent Alice away to the sea-side for change of air. She had tended her aunt very unweariedly, and the close confinement had begun to tell upon her health. A place on the southern coast was recommended, and Mrs. Scrymgeour—who since Aunt Amiel's illness, had installed herself as chaperone to Miss Grey—selected Brighton, taking into account with admirable prudence and foresight its vicinity to the small town where her nephew was just then fixed.

They went in the middle of January, intending to remain a fortnight or three weeks, if Aunt Amiel did not appear to feel Alice's absence too much, and return in time for the Festival, which was to take place some time during the month of February. Cuthbert had again been summoned southwards to be a substitute for his clerical friend. He would be in the neighbourhood during most of their stay, and Mrs. Scrymgeour trusted to his frequent intercourse with Alice so to cement the attachment between them, that it might speedily ripen into the union on which she had fixed her mind.

CHAPTER XV.

AND how was David Bruce faring through all this winter?

The long strife was over now. Fortune had been tardy in opening her golden doors, but she gave him entrance at last. His Oratorio was well received in London. The leading journals spoke of it as a complete success, a brilliant and unquestioned triumph. The best musical circles received him into their midst; titled people, not a few, found their way to those quiet little chambers of his in St. Clement's Inn: from many a silken-curtained boudoir and gilded saloon aristocratic voices warbled forth the exquisite solos and chorales of "Jael," and its composer, had he so chosen, might have been night after night the idol of Belgravian drawing-rooms, or the star of fashionable *soirèes musicales*. His fame reached Alice amidst the brilliance and glare of her Brighton life. With a shy, proud sort of pleasure, she read his praise in the public prints, and filled her little pocket-book with admiring "notices" cut from the principal musical papers. But she never spoke of him to Cuthbert Scrymgeour. Ever since that September evening when the "person" had been ignominiously dropped on the Norlands road, Cuthbert had avoided any mention of David Bruce; nor was it likely now, when the St. Olave's organist was a man no longer to be ignored, but envied, that the subject should be renewed. So Alice thought her own thoughts, and pondered over her own little memories, and held fast in her child heart the remembrance of this man, whose influence had been unconsciously the awakener of her life.

Over and over again the Oratorio of "Jael" was performed before crowded London audiences, under the conductorship of its composer; and then came applications for its performance in the "provinces," as the metropolitans call that geographical district which has the misfortune to lie outside their own centre of civilization. Requests came, too, from some of the great musical cities on the Continent, but these, for the present, David Bruce declined. After the first great success, one thought ever lay in his heart, one desire shaped itself steadily out above all ambitious schemes or longings; and this thought, this desire was, that at the Festival of St. Olave's, Alice Grey might listen to his Oratorio. And so, indeed, it was.

The good folks of the little Cathedral city of St. Olave's were somewhat scandalized at the sudden and brilliant success of the Scottish alien who had come and settled himself down amongst them. They had rather his laurels had been won more quietly, with more judicious decorum. They had no notion of people, especially strangers, leaping at one bound to the top of the social ladder; or, indeed, presuming to set foot there at all, unless born to the position. The rank and status of the Bruce family had long ago been decided in solemn conclave by the Position Committee, and, to say the least, it was annoying, if not humiliating, to be constrained to reconsider the verdict, and, after all, leave cards at Westwood. Still, on the other hand, St. Olave's had a reputation for good taste in the fine art line, and it would never do to ignore a production upon which London audiences had set the seal of their approval. If only the metropolis had received "Jael" coolly, or with a judicious amount of moderated approbation, then the Cathedral city might have preserved its dignity intact, nor been constrained to do homage to a man who owned neither descent nor position. But the teeming thousands of Exeter Hall and St. James's, had given the key-note of public opinion, and the provinces must follow in their train.

St. Olave's was slow, very slow, in awarding honour on its own responsibility. Deliberateness came next to descent in its social creed. If a man came down from town with the ticket of merit sewed to his coat, and printed withal in clear, unmistakable characters, well and good. St. Olave's was quite ready to endorse the opinions of the metropolis in matters of art, and could trot along, with wondrous correctness, over a ready-made tramway. But the brightest genius in the world, who came to it unknown and unrecommended, might wait at the doors of its respectability long enough before his talents procured him either fame or five-pound notes. Most likely, had this much-talked-of Oratorio been performed for the first time, before a select assembly of the Close families, it would have fallen quietly to the ground, never to rise again; but, having won its own place and gained its own renown, the St. Olave's people decided, after much deliberation, to rally round the composer, and say to the world at large, "See how we appreciate genius! See how we recognize the glorious birthright of intellect." Well done, Cathedral city of St. Olave's!

And so, one chill January morning, as David Bruce sat over his solitary breakfast in those dim little Clement's Inn chambers, a document was handed to him bearing the St. Olave's Cathedral crest—a padlock and golden key—and signed by the proper authorities. In which document Mr. Bruce was requested to do the city of St. Olave's the honour of conducting his Oratorio of "Jael" at the approaching Musical Festival. Moreover, he was informed that, as a mark of the honour which the city wished to confer upon so distinguished a composer, the fourth day—the great day of the Festival, the day sacred to aristocracy and the county families—would be reserved for his convenience.

David Bruce would have been something more, or perhaps something less than a man, if, as he read this important missive, stiff as it was with civic and ecclesiastical dignity, a flush of pardonable pride had not passed over his rugged face. But the pride soon faded out, and there came in its place the quiet light of content, the grand, sweet consciousness of hope fulfilled; not ambitious hope, not the greed of name, or fame, or gain, but the hope that lies nearer the heart of a true man than any of these—the hope which nestles upon the altar of hearth and home, and seeks neither gold nor glory, but only love, to keep it ever warm and bright.

So it was arranged that "Jael" should be performed in the Hall of Guild at the approaching grand Musical Festival; and, if the spirits of the departed are permitted to revisit the earth, that majestic piece of Hebrew womanhood might have walked the streets of St. Olave's, and seen her name, in letters as long as a man's arm, at every corner and turning of the old city.

David Bruce went to London, that grey December morning, an unknown man—nothing but a man. No hand save Janet's was stretched out for a farewell clasp. As he leaned back on the hard and not over-clean panels of the railway carriage, and wrapped his well-worn Highland tartan over his wasted form, no voice but hers cheered him; and her face, in its pale, quiet patience, was the only one which had any smile for him. He came back one of the great composers of his time, a man whom the world delighted to honour; before him, fame, wealth, success; behind him, the memory of toil overpast and triumph achieved; behind him, too, and far enough away now, all the scorn, and quiet contempt, and misappreciation against which he had battled so long.

Yes; it was very amusing to note how the worthy denizens of the Position Committee readjusted the social relations of David Bruce and his sister. Alice Grey's card had lain like a solitary nest-egg, lonely and unprotected in the little *papier-maché* tray on the table in the centre of the Westwood parlour. Now others, not a few, were deposited around it, promising at no distant period to hatch a goodly brood of acquaintance. Those of the Dean's lady and Elene Somers were the first to make their appearance; next came Mrs. Scrymgeour's, sent in an envelope all the way from Brighton; then that of the Canon-in-Residence; and ere a month of David's fame had elapsed, each of the Close families had left a pasteboard representative of its extreme friendliness. Mr. Bruce and his quiet sister no longer walked the Cathedral Close unrecognized—nay more, avoided. Aristocratic hands were held out to clasp theirs, and even the Bishop himself thought it not scorn to traverse the smooth green sward of that sacred enclosure, side by side with a man who had lunched with dukes and dined with gartered peers.

It was astonishing too, the different construction which the polite world began to put upon Mr. Bruce's habits and general demeanour. What used to be "such insufferable brusquerie," was now only manly indifference; that rare gift of silence, so fast inwrought into his nature and erewhile stigmatized as "boorish awkwardness and stupidity," turned out to be nothing but dignified reserve, perfectly natural in a man of such exalted talent, and on the whole rather fascinating than otherwise. Success in life is a wonderful help towards making manifest the latent excellencies of a man's character. It is like the translucent wave, which, washing over some dry bit of agate, brings out its rosy tints and azure veinings. By-and-by it even seemed that this ungainly Scotch pebble, so long stranded high and dry upon the barren sands, might be counted not unmeet to wear a golden setting, and take its place amongst the polished gems of the social collection; for prudent Close mammas no longer forbade their marriageable daughters to promenade the vicinity of Westwood Cottage, or cautioned them against the slightest approach to friendly relations with the staid, quiet, exceedingly unstylish looking lady who crossed the Close weekly on her way to the almshouses.

It was the night of David Bruce's return from London.

Ah, what a pleasant coming home that was! How cosy the little parlour looked, bathed in the warm red fire light; how tempting the genuine Scottish array of scones and crisp brown oat-cake which Tibbie had spread out on the damask covered table; and the old Scotchwoman herself, so different to the draggled London housemaid,—with her snow-white frilled cap, tied down with black ribbon, her kerchief of checkered gingham, her grey linsey sabbath gown, put on in honour of the "Maister,"—how she seemed to link the household with those long-ago Perth days, whose memory was so green and fragrant still.

David Bruce did not come back from London empty-handed as he went. The little portmanteau, capacious enough for all his worldly goods on the southern journey, was accompanied homewards by a stout portly trunk, which was dragged in and unpacked by Janet on the hearth-rug after tea, whilst David sat in his great arm-chair and watched the process. Only before she began, he took out and laid carefully away in his own desk, a tiny little morocco case, such as jewellers keep their treasures in.

There was a great burnous cloak of their own clan-tartan for his sister; he had ransacked half the shops in Oxford Street to find it, for amongst the few things Janet ever longed after, was a skreed of the Bruce plaid, just to wear for the sake of Auld Lang Syne. Once only since they came to St. Olave's, had she seen any of it; and that was a magnificent silk dress in a shop in the High Street, six months ago. She went in and asked the price, but came out again unsatisfied; seven guineas was too much to pay for the privilege of wearing the colours of her "ain countree." Her face brightened now, then saddened with the thought of dead friendships, as she shook out the cloak's long sweeping folds, and recognized the old colours that they used to wear when they were children scampering over the Perth Inches,—deep red, crossed with bands of green and white, and a single checker of yellow, the royal colour which a clansman is so proud to claim for his own. David wrapped it round her, and made her walk up and down the room.

"You shall be a braw leddie, yet, Jean," he said, smiling, but the smile and the thoughts that brought it were not all for his sister.

Besides the cloak, there was a beautifully wrought terra-cotta vase for the bow window, some little Parian statuettes to match the one of Beethoven, that stood upon the piano, and a few household belongings which careful Janet had commissioned him to purchase; for they found St. Olave's a terribly dear place as regarded house-keeping. Tibbie was not forgotten either. The sturdy old serving woman well nigh melted into tears when she was summoned "ben" to receive the plaidie, which her master had brought all the way "fra the big toun."

"Ye were aye a gude thochtfu' laddie for them as wanted the siller, Maister Davit," she said, curtseying in the doorway, "and the Lord send that ye sall wed a bonnie wee wifie, for ye're over leal an' true to live yer lane i' the world."

Janet did not hear the last words, for she was still bending over the memorial tartan, with a face full of thoughts; but they brought a colour deep as any maiden's blush to David's brow.

And then when all was cleared away, the brother and sister sat down side by side in the pleasant fire twilight. Mrs. Edenall was away to-night; she had gone to some public meeting that was being held in St. Olave's, because, as she said, the continued stillness of the cottage wearied her.

But Janet knew she had slipped away that they might have a quiet time to themselves after their long parting. Her absence was just one of those little bits of true-hearted tenderness which gleamed out now and then like winter flowers through the frost and snow of that unchangeable reserve of hers.

They said but little. David and his sister were always very undemonstrative in their household ways. It was a great rest to them though to be together again. In the long intervals of silence, Janet looked lovingly into her brother's face, pleased to note how the sharp worn lines of illness had faded out, and the grey eyes won back their own dear quietness. Nay, more than their own quietness, for to-night they seemed to shine with a deep inner light which she had never seen there before.

"How well he looks," she thought. "This visit to London has done him so much good; he will soon be quite strong again." And then she pictured to herself years and years of quiet home life with him, none but just they two together,—"my brother and I."

The January wind was crooning through the trees in Westwood Lane, sometimes rising into a blast that shook the ivy leaves against the trellised window, sometimes dying off into a low eerie wail almost like the dirge that moaned in stormy nights from the Cathedral belfry.

"Alice Grey has a dree time for her journey," Janet said at last.

David turned sharply round.

"You never told me she was away."

"No, for I had so many things to say; but she only set off this morning. Wasn't it strange, Davie, that you should pass each other on the road and never know it? You look sorry, brother, but she'll not be away at the Festival. Miss Luckie told me that Alice quite intended being home the night before "Jael" was to be performed. She has gone to Brighton."

"To Brighton; surely she was not ill?"

"No, only a wee bit pale, and not quite so springy as she used to be before you went away. She was aye tending Mrs. Grey, and it wearied her, Davie; she's a tender-hearted little thing." And then Janet began to speak of "poor Aunt Amiel," and told David all about her illness and Alice's loving, patient care.

He did not say anything. It seemed as if all the sunlight had faded suddenly from his thoughts. So many pleasant fancies had clustered round that expected meeting time. Over and over again he had pictured her bright smile of greeting, and her fresh, frank, girlish ways as she spoke to him of the triumph he had won. He turned his head away, shading his face with one hand. Janet thought he was tired, and so let him rest.

Still, after all, he remembered it was only for a little while, just a week or two, no more, and they should stand face to face once again, even as they had stood in that same room three months ago. Except that now they should stand free and equal; he a noble man and faithful, not uncrowned with that laurel wreath of honour, which he had only striven to win because, wearing it, the world would count him more worthy of her.

CHAPTER XVI.

THE Festival drew rapidly on, and the good folks of St. Olave's began to set themselves in right earnest to the various rites that preceded its advent. The people—meaning by these the working bees of the community, between whom and the "Close families" there yawned a gulf as impassable as that which the Roman Curtius gave his life to close—got their houses "done up," and put out notices of "Apartments to let" in the front windows. Careful housewives, who longed to turn an honest penny of pinmoney, counted over their stores of sheets and blankets, and speculated on the number of beds that could be made available for lodgers.

Every habitable tenement in the place, from the magnificent Royal Hotel itself, at which the Queen and Royal family had once partaken of biscuits and wine, thereby lifting the place into undying fame, down, or rather up, to the meanest little attic that could by possibility be coaxed into accommodating a stray tripper, was put into its best attire, thoroughly scoured, whitewashed, and purified.

Looked at in a sanitary point of view, a Festival is quite equal to a visitation of cholera, besides having this advantage, that it combines pleasure with utility, which thing cannot be affirmed of the other epidemic. Once in three years, at any rate, the city of St. Olave's underwent a complete visitation, from which it emerged fresh and sunshiny as a New York little boy on Thanksgiving-day morning. And, on this occasion, possibly because the citizens had just touched extreme high-water mark of the tide of progress, or because they wished to do special honour to the composer of the new Oratorio, the preliminaries were carried on with an unprecedented vehemence. The star of the charwoman was in the ascendant; grocers noticed a brisk demand for soda and fuller's earth, and if all England had only had the good sense to follow the example of St. Olave's, the soap market would no longer have been chronicled in the daily papers as "flat."

Votive clouds of dust—sweet incense offered at the shrine of the goddess of cleanliness—rose morning by morning from the Northgate Stray, a large field appropriated by civic grant to the beating of the city carpets. Paperers and white-washers were almost run off their feet, and as for chimney-sweeps, those sooty invaders of matutinal naps, they became positively coquettish, and treated their old customers with as much caprice as the reigning belle of the season thinks fit to lavish on her beseeching cavaliers. Washer-women's back yards presented a scene of bustling activity. Muslin window-curtains and bed-hangings of every conceivable shape and variety, fluttered from the lines and spread their snowy pinions to the passing breeze. Mrs. Marris was "pretty nigh beat out," as she expressed it, with nothing but blinds and counterpanes, although that ecclesiastical laundress proudly ignored the claims of "people," and restricted herself to the purification of Close family linen.

As the great event drew on, the fashionable drapery establishments in the upper quarter of the city, blossomed into unwonted splendour. Satins, rich, soft, and downy, displayed their blooming tints behind the plate-glass windows of the High Street; self-supporting moire antiques, from dowager brown to bridal white, bristled beside them; and silks, flounced, figured, and plain, shamed the rainbow for lustre. These were for the married aristocracy, the leading courses, so to speak, of the great social entertainment. Then, mingling with them, like the *entremêts* and fancy dishes, were floating ærial gauzes and tarlatanes, silver-starred muslins and filmy tulle illusions which seemed woven of air and moonshine, or cut in twenty-yard lengths from the webs of rose-tinted clouds, out of which the wardrobe of Aurora is popularly supposed to be replenished. And for the milliners' shops—ah! but it would need a pen steeped in Castalian dews to describe those temples of Flora, with their wreaths and knots and bouquets, their scarlet holly-berries and luscious damask roses for thc brunette's tawny brow, their blue-eyed forget-me-nots, lilies, and snowdrops for the sunny tresses of the blonde, their starry jasmine flowers for the young maiden's first ball, their wreaths of pouting orange blossom for the bride, the circlets of golden wheat and crimson cornflower waiting to bind the temples of some placid, dark-eyed matron, and vine leaves with their purple clusters and silver tendrils for bland, middle-aged dignity.

The all-important week arrived. The Festival placards increased in size and magnificence. "Jael," "Eli," and "Solomon," in golden letters a yard long, figured side by side with the names of the distinguished London *artistes* who were to sing their praises in the Hall of Guild. Early in the week the county families arrived. Fashionable-looking men, with retreating chins and finely-chiselled noses, lounged in the Cathedral stalls at service-time, or smoked their cigars at the doors of the Royal Hotel. Imperial women floated slowly down the narrow old-fashioned streets, women whose every step and gesture proclaimed the centuries of Norman blood that coursed their veins, and whose voices had that fine, clear, musical ring which betokens the old English nobility. Mingling with them, too—for the railway companies would persist in getting up cheap trips from the manufacturing districts—tramped frowsy-faced, freckled, honest-eyed mill girls, with astounding bonnets and yellow cotton gloves; dependable girls, nevertheless, who albeit they brought not much beauty into it, might do as much good in the world as their clear-skinned Norman sisters. And, to those long steeped in the reticence and *nil admirari* repose of the little Cathedral city, it was somewhat refreshing to mark the gusto with which these unschooled children of machinery blurted out their astonishment at the grand old Minster, or relieved their excited feelings by frantic nudges of delight administered to the protruding elbows of the broad-shouldered swains who accompanied them.

Amongst this motley throng, the professionals were easily to be recognized. They came from all parts, for the St. Olave's Festival held no mean place in the musical world. There were Germans, light-haired, pale-faced, with volumes of philosophical speculations brooding beneath their sleepy eyelids; dapper, white-handed little Frenchmen, who broke the hearts of the barmaids at the Royal Hotel with their roguish smiles and curled imperials; and, stealing through the dim Cathedral aisles, or curiously peering round the crumbling arches of the Monastery, were swarthy Italians with fathomless glittering eyes which made one shiver to look into them, so eloquently did they speak of midnight and stilettoes.

As the city filled, and the quiet little streets grew noisy with the tramp of stranger feet and the clatter of foreign tongues, Mrs. Edenall became nervous, almost excited, at times. Regularly, morning by morning, she went to the Minster and looked eagerly at the lengthening list of visitors' names in the book which was kept at the entrance of the north aisle, and then she would pace up and down the nave, peering restlessly into one and another of the hundreds of strange faces which met her. There was one very quiet seat, behind the canopied monument of Alfric, first Bishop of St. Olave's. It was out of sight of passers-by, but overlooked the whole length of the nave and south transept. Here she would sit for hours, watching patiently for the one face that never came, until her own grew weary and hopeless; and then, as the great bell sounded for the closing of the doors, she turned away with hands tightly clenched, and a step that grew daily more feeble.

Every afternoon, too, as the up-train from Edinburgh passed through the station, she might be seen at the window of the ladies' waiting-room, anxiously gazing through the thick wire-blinds at the groups of stalwart men and noble women who turned out upon the platform.

And so the week wore on until Thursday, the third day of the Festival. On Tuesday and Wednesday there had been grand Oratorio performances in the Hall of Guild, but this evening the programme was varied by a full dress miscellaneous concert, at which the prima donna of Covent Garden was to make her first appearance in St. Olave's, sustained by a cluster of musical celebrities, such as had never been gathered together before on any but a London orchestra.

Janet Bruce sat by the fire in the parlour at Westwood, knitting away at her little white socks, just as quietly and patiently as ever. Perhaps her face might be a shade brighter now, for she was proud of her brother's success, and she was looking forward rather eagerly to his triumph—for she knew it would be a triumph—at the performance of "Jael" next evening. David had been hard at work all day preparing the choristers for their parts, and after coming home for a hasty dinner, had set off again to evening service at the Minster.

The room looked very peaceful in the deepening twilight of that early February evening. Not a change had been made in the simplicity, almost frugality of its furniture. Everything remained as it had been in the time of their poverty and obscurity. The well-worn crimson carpet, the old embroidered table-cover, with its border of armorial bearings, so dim and faded now, the drab moreen curtains edged with a quaker-like binding of black velvet, such as one sees in century-old country houses; there was nothing grand or artistic in the room, but that carved oak frame with its fanciful clusters of leaves and flowers heaped over arabesques of quaint device. But there were no flame shadows now to play hide-and-seek upon it, for the fire had burned down to a deep, steady, red glow, which made the room seem stiller than ever.

Mrs. Edenall was there. She seemed restless and excited. She paced rapidly up and down the room like some caged animal that is longing for space and liberty. It was a habit she had brought with her to Westwood, but of late she had almost given it up, much to Janet's secret satisfaction. Whenever an irritable or nervous mood came upon her, she took to it again, and for the last few days the little time that she staid indoors, had been almost entirely spent in this restless wandering to and fro. Her hands were clasped, her teeth set together, and when at every turn she reached the wall, she looked fiercely at it, as though she longed to shatter it down and dash out into the free, open air. It grieved Janet to see how the lull which once seemed to have come over this strange woman's spirit had entirely passed away, and all the old fever and weariness come back. But she bore with it patiently, never asking the why or wherefore.

At length Mrs. Edenall paused with an angry, impatient gesture.

"Miss Bruce," she said, "I cannot stay here any longer; the stillness of this room wearies me—it kills me. I shall go to the Cathedral prayers, the music will not be over yet."

"What, this wretched afternoon?" said Janet, and not without cause, for the sleet was driving against the windows, and the wind screamed wildly at intervals through the leafless branches of the old elm trees in Westwood Lane.

"Oh!" replied Mrs. Edenall, with a touch of the old careless scorn, "you know I am not given to indulging in colds; the weather has no effect upon me."

And that was true. She seemed to have a charm against chills and agues. She would go out amid drenching rain and driving snow, which would have sown the seeds of consumption in any but an iron-strong frame; but it seemed as if disease, physical disease, at least, had no work to do for her.

"And," she continued, "I shall most likely look into the concert afterwards, so do not wonder if I am late."

"But surely, Mrs. Edenall, you will not go to the concert alone, and David said he should not be there to-night, he will be so tired when he comes home from the service."

"Thank you; I don't care about Mr. Bruce's company. I shall be quite safe. No one ever does me any harm, and as for looking strange, I have given over thinking about that."

And as she said this she shook her head back with that wild, careless sort of grace, which reminded Janet so unaccountably of Alice Grey's manner sometimes; except that in Alice the gesture only betrayed a certain girlish thoughtlessness, and in Mrs. Edenall it conveyed the impression of such utter pride and scorn.

Janet made no further remark, and Mrs. Edenall went out of the room. She wrapped herself in a long grey frieze cloak, which reached nearly to her feet, tied a thick Shetland veil over her crape bonnet, and then sallied forth into the chill February gloom.

The wind swirled wildly down the narrow streets, drifting the sleet into her face, and almost blinding her. But she did not seem to heed it. She walked quickly, impetuously on, as though striving to outstrip or conquer some evil influence that had come down upon her. It was quite dark before she reached the Minster. The light from the brilliantly-illuminated choir flickered faintly through the clerestory windows, half hiding, half revealing the sculptured figures and the highly-wrought fret-work of the stone mouldings above. It was long past six o'clock and the service was more than half over, so instead of going into the choir to her usual seat near the prebendary stalls, she went into the side aisle and sat down on the base of an old monument near the little stair that led to the organ. It was a grotesque old piece of sculpture to the memory of Sir Roger de Botolph, a knight of the sixteenth century, and Dame Dorothy, his spouse. The worthy folks were kneeling face to face beneath an elaborate canopy, apparently saying their prayers to each other. Between them was a death's head and cross bones; above, a lengthy Latin inscription recorded their respective alms-deeds and benefactions to the Church. Three little girls in starched ruffs, and as many little boys in hose and doublets, the "infantry," as the inscription stated, of Sir Roger and Dame Dorothy, were ranged in a line behind their father and mother, having their hands clasped, and wearing a solemn aspect of countenance.

A happy family doubtless they had been in their time; all dead now, and gone to heaven let us hope. And it was beside this stone memento of peaceful domestic unity that Mrs. Edenall, the lonely, friendless woman, sat and listened in a sort of waking dream to the pealing tones of the organ.

The Cathedral music was always very choice during the Festival, for strangers came from all parts to hear it. This afternoon it was a selection from Mozart's Twelfth Mass, adapted to English words. People came in and out during the whole service; some just strolling into the choir for a few minutes to listen to the music and out again; some examining and copying the monumental brasses; some with guide-book and spectacles, viewing the architectural beauties of the place; some—very few though—standing with bowed head and reverent aspect as in the presence of Him to whom that grand temple belonged.

Just as the chanting of the Psalms was over, Cuthbert Scrymgeour and a military-looking gentleman strolled up the aisle and paused near to where Mrs. Edenall sat. She did not know who they were, indeed she knew scarcely anybody in St. Olave's. She could hear distinctly, however, all they said, for the conversation was not carried on in the most subdued of tones. The Reverend Cuthbert was evidently of opinion that the fact of standing a few inches outside the choir screen, completely absolved him from all need of partaking in, or even recognizing the service which was going on within its sacred enclosure.

"You'll be at the concert to-night, Scrymgeour, of course," said the military friend.

"Why, no, Madden. I'm afraid not. I should like uncommonly to drop in for half-an-hour or so, but you see my charmer is coming home from Brighton to-night, and I must do the polite at the Old Lodge."

"Quite right. It will never do for Euterpe to put Erato's nose out of joint, we all know that. You're a lucky fellow Scrymgeour; the little Grey girl is as pretty a piece of feminine witchery as I've seen for a good while. By the way, when are you going to be turned off?"

"Oh, not just yet," and Cuthbert stroked his whiskers. "A fellow can't be expected to give up his freedom, and turn into a Benedict all at once, eh?"

"Exactly. I was rather surprised when I heard you had been and gone and done the preliminaries in such a bustle. Afraid of some one else stepping in before you, I suppose. Half thought of making a try myself once, after that pic-nic, but you see married life doesn't do for the army."

Just then the clergyman began to intone the Creed. Had Cuthbert Scrymgeour been standing at his place in the choir, he would have salaamed until his Grecian nose scraped the ledge of the reading desk. Under present circumstances he did not consider such a mark of respect binding upon his conscience, and as the rustle of priestly vestments in the choir marked the utterance of the Name at which every knee shall bow, he stood idly quizzing the groups of loungers and tapping his polished boots with a silver-mounted ebony cane.

Their vacant gossip jarred upon Mrs. Edenall. She moved away from her seat and went into the nave, quite away down to the west end where scarce a footstep was stirring save her own. There, at least, all was solemn and calm and still. People rave over the majesty of continental Cathedral interiors, but travellers who had "done" all the architectural wonders of Europe, came home and confessed that none of them surpassed, or even equalled St. Olave's Cathedral in the twilight of winter time. She stood beneath the statue niches which supported the arch of the great west window. From the lofty clustered columns which spanned the entrance to the choir, a flood of light poured over the transepts and the eastern end of the nave, growing fainter and fainter as it passed column after column, until at last it spent itself in a feeble flicker upon the richly foliated tracery of the west window. The side aisles were in deep gloom, only a stray light here and there suggesting, but not outlining, the grand clustered pillars whose flowered capitals were hidden in complete darkness. Here and there a gleam of light from the choir revealed a fragment of some majestic arch, or pencilled out upon the marble walls the shadows of the curiously wrought bosses that hung from the groined roof. But all seemed vast and disjointed and fragmentary, like the human soul itself, unlit by the daylight of truth.

For sometime Mrs. Edenall was alone. Then she heard footsteps, and by-and-by a tall figure wrapped in a plaid, crossed and re-crossed the aisle not far away from where she stood. In the deep shadow she could scarcely distinguish his form, much less the contour of his face, but the step was that of a large, heavily-made man. As he came nearer to her, the choir lights were extinguished, leaving the building in complete darkness, except where a single lamp burned over the south entrance. Then the voice of the verger was heard echoing through the building—"Strangers out." She made her way across the aisle, and to avoid the jostling crowd who thronged the great doors, stole out through a little narrow entry which led into the Close from the west end.

Sleet and wind had it all their own way in the Close to-night. It wanted half an hour yet to the opening of the Concert Hall doors, and the carriages had not yet begun to draw up at the tall, old-fashioned houses that loomed so gray and ghostly in the evening gloom. A pleasant rosy glow came from the crimson curtained windows of the Old Lodge, and gleamed through the leafless branches of the trees that skirted the garden. It spoke of home, and rest, and comfort, and Mrs. Edenall turned passionately away from it—the very thought seemed to mock her. She could not return to Westwood. Its never changing stillness was insufferable. She was in that state of mind when quiet produces almost madness. She gathered her cloak round her and walked fiercely up and down the Close, until she was quite exhausted; and then leaning against one of the projecting buttresses of the west tower, she watched the sleet go drifting by.

Its incessant motion, quick, aimless, uncertain, and yet so silent, seemed to soothe her. She looked at it until a sort of magnetic quietness came over her. As the Minster bells struck half-past seven she turned away towards the Concert Hall. A crowd was already thickening around it, and a long line of carriages drawing up at the private door which conducted to the reserved seats. Groups of dirty little children and haggard pale-faced girls were huddled together near the canvas awning that had been erected over the pavement, giving vent to pent-up whispers of envious amazement as some fair-haired belle, in silver-sprigged tulle, alighted from her carriage and floated up the brilliantly-lighted staircase, or a stout old dowager bristling in moir antique and family diamonds, sailed majestically out of sight.

Mrs. Edenall passed this door and went to the

promenade entrance. She had some difficulty in making her way through the thickening mass of people that blocked up the lobbies and corridors, and by the time she reached the hall, all the best seats were already taken. But she did not care for hearing. All she wanted was to see. After long patient waiting, she forced a passage to the side seats, and got a place behind one of the massive columns that supported the gallery, from which, almost unseen herself, she could look out over the whole room; from the reserved seats, already blossoming into a perfect parterre of wreaths and bouquets, past the sedater splendours of the middle floor, chiefly filled by retired trades-people in somewhat seedy half-dress, to the moving groups of the promenade; a confused mass of strangers, foreigners, and aliens, chiefly men, with here and there a shabbily dressed woman or two, all elbowing, jostling, and pushing their way towards the low, crimson-covered barricade, which protected the upper and second rate sociality of St. Olave's from the *ignobile vulgus* of the five shilling seats.

CHAPTER XVII.

THE room began to fill. Carriage after carriage poured its dazzling contribution into the full-dress seats; like a distant sound of waves the thickening footsteps echoed and re-echoed along the wide corridors. By-and-by the whole place was packed. From her sheltered nook, Mrs. Edenall peered eagerly out, but the face she sought never came. Sometimes amidst the surging mass beneath and around her, one like it would appear, and then she leaned forward with keen hungry gaze, but only to fall back more wearily again as the fancied resemblance resolved itself into the blank features of some stranger countenance.

The musicians came on the orchestra, stealing with slow noiseless steps to their places, their sombre costumes contrasting vividly with the banners emblazoned with heraldic devices, the draperies of crimson velvet, the wreaths and festoons of shining evergreens. Then came the tuning of instruments, twang after twang of violin strings mingled now and then with the deep sound of a violoncello or a clear solitary pianoforte note. Presently a round of applause announced the debût of the professionals who were to commence the performance—four dark quiet gentlemanly-looking men, with that set, everlasting smile and cool nonchalance of deportment which becomes so habitual to public characters, especially musicians.

The first piece was a quartett for stringed instruments. Mrs. Edenall scarcely listened to it. That long, long gaze of mute inquiry over and disappointed, she had drawn her veil tightly over her face, and leaned her head against the marble column at her side, with the utterly weary spiritless air of one who can neither suffer nor enjoy anything. After the quartett came a pianoforte solo, a grand frothy fly-away sort of thing, introduced like the "padding" in a popular magazine to make a setting for the more talented contributions. When this was over, the leading article, the Covent Garden prima donna, made her appearance.

She was a grand, queenly woman, standing like a white-robed statue, pure and passionless, amidst the admiring multitude. There was no flattered vanity, scarce even the semblance of recognition, in the slight and graceful gesture with which she acknowledged the peals of tumultuous greeting that rang through the Hall of Guild. She seemed to stand apart from the gaping fashionable throng in some thought world of her own, from which upon the deep silence that followed the first welcome, she let fall, calmly and almost unconsciously, drops of music, tender, soft, and peaceful as those we hear in dreams.

Mrs. Edenall could not but listen now. All Europe had hushed its play to hear that voice. Sometimes its tones were passionate and pleading as though born from infinite deeps of sorrow; sometimes they trickled merrily along with no more measured art than that which guides the ripples of a mountain stream; sometimes they flashed out into sudden brilliance, like a fountain springing skywards and tossing the sunlight from each of its myriad drops; then trembling away down into a low sweet murmur that was rather heard than felt, so gently, so patiently it stole into the listening heart.

She ceased. They called her back with shouts of rapture. Calmly, proudly she came, and then without any accompaniment, without a single shake, or grace, or artistic flourish, she sang the English ballad, "Home, sweet Home."

That familiar song, the national anthem of every English heart, the psalm of every English fireside! The song that mothers croon to their sleeping babes; that falls like a benediction on the soldier's ear as he lies in snow-covered hut or hospital ward. The song that brings tears, soft and childlike, to the prodigal's eye when its music smites him in the land of strangers, and makes the poor street cast-away crouch pale and repentant before the memories it brings. The song that fills every husband's heart with honest pride; the first song we learn to love, the last we learn to forget. "Home, sweet Home." Alas! for those, who listening to its strains find in them only the stinging remembrance of joys that can never, never come again!

"Allow me to pass. I did not know it was so late," said a deep-toned voice a few benches behind where Mrs. Edenall was sitting.

The speaker was a tall finely-made man. His garb and aspect would have betrayed his nationality, even had not the steady Scottish accent with which he spoke done it for him. He wore a tartan plaid, chiefly red, checkered with black and white, wrapped round him after that negligent fashion which only born Highlanders know how to manage, and dangling from his ungloved right hand was a Glengarry bonnet of the same tartan. He was very broad and stalwart, of the genuine Caledonian build, with great tangling masses of curling flaxen hair swept back from a high, well-shaped forehead. He might be forty-five, perhaps more, perhaps less, but men with light hair look young so long. It is only the strong dark-locked nature that betrays the iron-grey grasp of time. His face was meant to be a noble one. He had the majestic leonine features, the aquiline nose, the keen piercing blue eyes of the thorough-born Scot. But the lower part of the face spoilt them all. Its expression was low and earthly. The lips, large and shapeless, were those of a man enslaved by pleasure, a man never wakened by any noble impulse or lofty purpose. That mouth gave the lie boldly and decidedly to the upper part of the face, and he did well to hide it by the crisp curls of a golden-red beard and moustache. Still in consideration of his face and figure altogether, he was what most people would call a very fine man.

"Allow me to pass," he repeated; and this time there was a touch of quick impatience in his voice.

Mrs. Edenall caught it. She turned wildly round, as though smitten by some unexpected blow. A cry of smothered excitement rose to her lips, but she had self-control enough to force it back. For a while she trembled violently, and but for the pillar at her side would have fallen to the ground. After pausing a moment or two, she rose, and, with very tottering steps, tried to make her way through the people.

The stranger was far ahead of her. He pushed

vigorously on, not sparing hard words, or even blows, when either would facilitate his passage. She followed as best she could. The corridors were completely wedged with people waiting to come in at reduced prices to the second part of the concert. Often, in the crowd, she lost sight of him; now a marble statue came between them, anon the blinding glare of a chandelier fell full upon her straining eyes, or he disappeared behind the folds of some crimson drapery. He had nearly reached the carriage road outside before she got to the door. She heard him hail a cab and shout to the driver—

"To the Royal Hotel—quick!"

She followed, pressing with desperate energy through the masses of low, loose, shabbily-dressed people that loitered within the railed yard, waiting to catch sight of the full-dress company.

"Laws! Missus, do be steady now, can't ye?" said one towering Irishwoman, whose red shawl she accidentally caught and almost tore it from the stout matron's shoulders. "Ain't there no pleecemen hereabouts to give an eye to drunken folk sich as the likes of ye?"

"Lost her beau! Take yer home for sixpence,

ma'am;" and a sidelong, leering-looking fellow pushed his greasy coat-sleeve in her face.

But she heeded neither jest nor insult, as she pressed frantically forward, threading her way through the network of carriages which blocked the street. Over and over again, the cabmen had to rein up their horses, or she would have been trodden to death. By-and-by the road became clearer, and nothing hindered her but the driving sleet. At last she reached the hotel. Two or three waiters were loitering about in the entrance, reading the newspapers and gossiping with each other. Carpet bags and portmanteaus were heaped up near the door, in readiness for visitors who had to leave after the concert was over.

"Well, ma'am, what may we have the honour of doing for you?" said one of the waiters, in a pert, confident tone. It was not a common thing for ladies to come alone to the Royal Hotel at that time of night, without luggage either, and no signs of travel about them.

"I wish to see Mr. Douglas Ramsay. I understand he is staying here."

She had thrown back her veil. Her face was ashen pale, but it had all the innate majesty which no sorrow or anxiety could outwear. And something in her voice or gesture awed the man, for he answered, quite respectfully—

"Mr. Douglas Ramsay, ma'am? I don't recollect the name, but I'll inquire. Take a seat, ma'am;" and he showed her into a little room on the right-hand side of the door.

One or two gentlemen were chatting at the further end, but they took no notice of her. She heard the waiter loudly calling the name she had given him, from landing to landing of the great staircase—the name which for years she had never heard—the name which she scarce had power to whisper to her own heart, save in the stillness of night and solitude. Presently the man came back.

"Mr. Ramsay left, ma'am, about five minutes ago. He was going off by the north train." And then, perhaps noticing the stony, despairing look that came into Mrs. Edenall's face, he added, glancing up at the great clock which stood on the staircase—

"You would soon catch him in a cab, ma'am; only there's none to be got to-night, because of the concert. But I shouldn't wonder, if you was to walk fast, you might be at the station afore the train was away. They're always behind-hand busy nights like these. It's not far, ma'am: up to the top of the High Street, and then take the first turning to the right; that'll lead you——"

The rest of his direction was given to the empty chair. Without waiting to thank him, Mrs. Edenall flew through the hall, down the wide flight of steps, and into the dark winding streets. On she went, with almost the speed of madness, past alley and postern, through crowded courts and deserted bye-lanes. Once only, under a crumbling archway of the old monastery, she paused for breath, just a moment, no more, and then on again, more wildly than before. The station was a little way out of the city. Ere she reached it, the bell rang; and when, at last, panting and weary, she sped through the iron gateway, the sharp sound of the railway whistle smote upon the air, and the north train wound slowly away from the platform, the fiery eyes of its two red signals glaring fiercely through the gloom.

With one more desperate effort she gathered up all her remaining energy and rushed after it.

As yet it moved leisurely, with a long, slow, snake-like trail. She ran past carriage after carriage, unperceived in the thickening darkness of night. Some were quite empty; in some was a single sleeper, muffled in great coat and comforter; some were crowded with jolly-looking men, laughing and smoking.

It was in the last carriage of all—a padded and cushioned first class—that the flickering lamplight fell upon that grand Highland head, with its coronal of waving flaxen hair.

No one else was in the compartment. Mr. Ramsay was wrapped in his plaid; on the vacant seat beside him lay his Glengarry bonnet and a flask of spirits. The *Times* lay on his knee; he seemed to be settling himself down to a comfortable study of it, just as any well-to-do gentleman might, with a full purse and a night's uninterrupted leisure.

With frenzied determination Mrs. Edenall sprang on the step and clung to the handle of the carriage.

"Douglas! Douglas Ramsay!" she muttered in a low, hoarse, sepulchral voice; she was too spent with wild excitement to shriek or cry.

The paper fell from his hands; he sprang to his feet. His countenance kindled into surprise, then into alarm, then into angry horror. Was that white ashen thing indeed a woman's face, or had it come from the land of ghosts, to call back his sin to his remembrance? Like a buried corpse, indeed, it looked, save for those great passionate grey eyes, with the mingled love and fury burning through them, and scorching into his very soul. He started back, stretching out his hands with a gesture of fear. She thrust hers into the carriage. A moment more and their fingers would have met—Ah, then in that wild frantic clasp, he would have felt no ghostly visitant had sought him out.

"Passengers not allowed to stand on the steps." said the guard, in a cool, collected, business-like voice; and with as much ease as if she had been a child, he unloosed her cold fingers from the carriage door, and lifted her to the ground.

And Douglas Ramsay's last look upon her was full of horror, and dread, and loathing; nothing but this. She had not even had time to curse him, or hurl one kiss of her pent-up love upon his lips.

With a low cry of despair, drowned as soon as it passed her lips by the sharp whistle of the now rapidly moving train, she crawled to the hedgeside, and fell down there, utterly spent and overworn; out of all that heaven and earth could give longing only for death, nothing but death.

CHAPTER XVIII.

HOW long she lay there beneath the driving sleet, she could not tell. When she came to herself again the moonlight was whitening the ragged edge of a great dim cloud that lay piled up against the horizon. The red and green lights of the station were gleaming a quarter of a mile away, and she could hear the heavy tramp of the engineers at work in the forges. She rose, aching in every limb, and went slowly homewards. When she had got about half way, she remembered a little lane that led past the Low Gardens into the Westwood Road. She turned into this to avoid going through the brightly-lighted streets of St. Olave's. She walked on as if in a brooding dream, too worn and desolate to feel anything acutely. All that she remembered of the past was a dim, aching sense of wrong and disappointment. Bodily weakness had mercifully dulled her mental powers, and held in abeyance the bitter pain that must come sooner or later to a nature like hers after the strain through which it had just passed.

About a hundred yards down the lane was the little meeting-house used by the Primitive Methodists. She had once passed it with Janet Bruce, and they had gone in to look round. It was lighted up now, as if for some service. The warm glow shining through the half-open door into the chill, dark night, lured her to the threshold.

"May I come in?" she said to the man who kept the door.

He seemed surprised that she should ask, and directed her into the room where the service was to be held. She crept behind the people to a form against the wall, partly screened by an open door which led to a little vestry beyond. There she sank down half fainting upon the low seat. She seemed to herself in a sort of vague, dead stupor; she had endured to the very verge of endurance; nothing worse could come now. The night could grow no darker, the next change must be the morning dawn.

By-and-by she woke from the swoon into which the sudden warmth of the room had thrown her, and began to look around this new resting-place that she had so unexpectedly found.

It was a square room, neither large nor lofty, but well-lighted, and exquisitely clean. The walls were coloured with a pleasant grey tint, soft and refreshing to the eye. White blinds were drawn over the square windows. The only decoration in the room was a narrow cornice of scroll pattern which bordered the flat panelled ceiling. On one side of the room was a platform raised about a foot from the floor; upon it stood a plain deal desk, with a bible and hymn-book for the use of the minister who conducted the service.

Facing this desk were two long rows of benches, divided by an aisle up the middle. The men sat on the right-hand, the women on the left. By the time the service began, there might be about a hundred present.

The women were chiefly aged, many of them in widow's weeds, most of them wearing mourning

Mrs. Cromarty sat on one of the front benches. She seemed to be wrapped in meditation, for her eyes were closed and a strange light shone out from her grand still face. The men evidently belonged to the working classes. Some of them were old and grey-headed, with bent shoulders and faces deeply scarred with the marks of care. Some were middle-aged, grave thoughtful-looking men with resolute faces and stalwart muscular frames; the sort of men who, if they had been sailors, would have perilled their lives to save a sinking ship; if firemen, would have walked calmly into the rack of a burning house so only duty sent them there; if colliers, would have braved fire-damp and foul air to fetch out a buried comrade. Still, steady men they were, with the make of a hero in every one of them. And some were stripling lads, apprentices who had dressed themselves after a day's work and come here for rest, body rest and soul rest. Looking round upon them all, noting their reverent demeanour, the hushed, girded expression of most of the countenances, you could not but have the impression that the religion of these people was very earnest and deep-seated; not a garb to be put on and off like Sunday clothing, but an influence that informed and nerved and intensified the whole life.

As the little clock over the platform struck nine, the minister took his place at the desk.

"Let us worship God."

All knelt down, and he offered a short, simple, fervent prayer, to which most of the men and some of the women responded from time to time with a vigour and heartiness that would have secured their immediate ejection from any other place of worship in St. Olave's.

After they rose from their knees, the minister read the twelfth chapter of the Epistle to the Romans, and then commenced his address. He leaned with folded arms over the desk, looking at one and another of his congregation, and sometimes smiling, as their eyes met his, with a beaming glance of recognition. He used neither pomp of words nor flow of oratory; he seemed like a man speaking to his companions in the quiet intercourse of home life.

"My friends," he said, "We have been brought to the close of another working day. We have come to this little meeting, some from our workshops, some from our counters, some from our firesides, and some—many I trust—from our places of prayer. God will not send us empty away. He has a blessing for each one of us, and He giveth liberally, upbraiding not. It may be that some of you have come here cast down and afflicted; if so, remember there is One standing in the midst of us who says, 'Come unto Me and I will give you rest.' He is very pitiful and of tender mercy, and He will lay no more upon you than you are able to bear. Others there may be who are toiling hard amidst the cares and anxieties of this life; sore wounded by the archers, yet striving to keep a conscience void of offence towards God and man. To such the Great Master says—'I know thy works.' Do not be afraid of duty. Make your daily duties part of your religion, and God will make them means of grace to your souls. Perhaps there are others who have come with the stain of unforgiven sin upon their consciences. You, my friends, are heartsick and weary, but Jesus is not far from any one of you. He has borne your sins and carried your sorrows; why, then, should you be burdened with them?

'Cast on Jesus all thy care,
Tis enough that He is nigh;
He will all thy burden bear,
He will all thy wants supply.

> 'He thy soul will safely lead,
> In His tender care confide;
> Call on Him in time of need,
> He will be thy guard and guide.'"

Then he spoke of the beauty and seriousness of life. "God," he said, "has a purpose for each one of us, and it should be the great aim of our lives to find out what this purpose is, and then in right earnest set ourselves to the realizing of it. We are often told that it is a serious thing to die; it would be well if we remembered that it is a far more serious thing to live. We will now sing a hymn, and afterwards those of you who feel drawn out to do so, will tell us of the dealings of God with your souls. Say what you have to say shortly and simply. God does not care for your much speaking; only see to it that you say it truly."

He then read out this hymn:—

> "I lay my sins on Jesus,
> The spotless Lamb of God;
> He bears them all, and frees us,
> From the accursed load.
>
> "I bring my griefs to Jesus,
> My sorrows and my fears;
> He from them all releases,
> He every burden bears.

"I rest my soul on Jesus,
This weary soul of mine;
His right hand me embraces,
I on His breast recline.

"I love the name of Jesus,
Emanuel, Christ, the Lord;
Like fragrance on the breezes,
His name abroad is poured."

After he had read the entire hymn, the minister gave it out by two lines at a time. One of the men near the desk started a tune and the others followed, joined presently by the tremulous treble voices of the women.

Mrs. Edenall's head drooped lower and lower; soon the tears trickled slowly, one by one, from beneath her thick veil. But people often wept at that service, and the woman by her side did not notice her, except by a single glance of quiet respectful sympathy with what she took to be a soul in communion with its Maker.

And so indeed it was.

After the hymn was over, there followed a long pause.

Then Mrs. Cromarty rose. Her hands were clasped together over her little hymn-book, her eyes uplifted, her whole face seemed brightened by an indwelling presence of stedfast joy.

"I'm very happy," she said. "I just feel I'm doing what Jesus wants me to do, and as I take it that's the most o' what folks need to carry them straight along through this world. He's got all my heart, inside an' out, it all belongs to Him, and He fills it with such a peace as I can't tell of. There's nothing in the world like loving the Lord Jesus. He's a good Master, and never keeps back a penny of the wages promised to them as serves him faithful. It was the best day's work I ever did when I got 'listed in among His people. He's been doing me good ever since. I can tell of it as well as if it was nobbut yesterday—first time I ever got a sight o' true religion. It's five-an'-thirty year come next Martinmas hiring, and I were tramping along London streets wi' scarce a rag to my back, just picking up a penny in selling bits o' shoe-laces and matches. I see'd a room lighted up, and, thinks I, it looks warm and comfortable like, I'll go in and sit me down. Mebby there's some poor body comed in here to-night because the room looks warm and comfortable. May the Lord Almighty meet 'em and do 'em a bit o' good to their precious souls."

In the hearty Amens which sealed this wish,

that which sighed out from Mrs. Edenall's lips was unheard—unheard, at least, by the visible worshippers in that little shrine. Mrs. Cromarty went on.

"I slipped my basket under t' seat, and started listening. Minister was agate with that beautiful parable about the Prodigal Son. He read it sort o' sweet and tender, summut as the Lord Jesus might ha' spoken it, an' it came over me like rain i' the summer-time, when things is withered wi' overmuch sunshine. Thinks I to myself, Honor Grant—it was afore I were married, a good bit—Honor Grant, if ever there's a prodigal in this world it's you. And then I kind o' heard a whisper in my heart—'Him that cometh unto me, I will in no wise cast out.' *And I came.*"

She paused awhile, for her voice was quivering with emotion, and the unshed tears were glistening in her great dark eyes. Then she began again—

"I get's tempted sometimes. I suppose people ain't never clear shut o' temptation i' this world. As long as there's a bit o' tinder left in the soul, Satan 'll try hard to strike a spark at it. But, bless the Lord, He brings me off conqueror, He does. 'Tisn't my strength as does it. I'm just nothing but a bruised reed, and I should clean snap in two if I hadn't His strength to hold on to. But He does keep me. He says to me, 'Fear not, I am with thee,' and then I get so happy I burst out singing. I was once a poor lone woman with never a friend to look to, and a heart so full of wickedness, that the blessed angels might have shuddered at it. Now the light's shone in upon me, and this is all my song—

'My God is reconciled,
His pardoning voice I hear,
He owns me for His child,
I can no longer fear.
With confidence I now draw nigh,
And Father! Abba Father! cry.'"

Mrs. Cromarty ceased, and there was deep, utter silence whilst the recording angel took that poor woman's hymn of praise and laid it on the steps of the great white throne.

The next speaker was an old man, feeble and palsied. He rose very slowly, steadying himself on a stout oaken staff which he held in both hands. His voice had a tone of unconscious patient grief, such as those use to whom sorrow has become not an accident but a habit, the prevailing key-note of their lives. He had to tell of bereavement. During that week his wife had died and been buried, and the old man was left alone. He spoke of her death, her last words, his great loneliness. The women sobbed as they heard his touching story, and one or two of the men wiped away a stray tear with their coat sleeves.

"I have no one to care for me now," he said, "my lass is gone; we'd lived and tewed together five-and-fifty year. Mebby I used to speak a bit sharp tull her sometimes; but I wouldn't do it now nobbut she could come back to me. Hard words turns into bitter stings when them we spoke 'em to is gone. And my childer's all dead too. My lass and me buried the last of em' two years gone. I sit by my bit o' fire all alone, and I'm oft tempted to say the Lord has dealt very bitterly with me. Then I ask for grace to be patient, and when I can nayther praise nor pray, I just tries to murmur out—'Thy will be done.' But it's a bitter cup."

He sat down. At that moment, quite suddenly, a woman from the far corner of the room began to sing in a low, sweet voice, soon joined by the other women and some of the men—

"My rest is in heaven, my rest is not here,
Then why should I murmur when trials are near?
Be hushed my dark spirit, the worst that can come,
But shortens my journey, and hastens me home.
Home! home! sweet home!
There's no place like heaven, there's no place like home."

They sang it to the tune of "Home, sweet Home," the same tune to which Mrs. Edenall had listened scarce more than an hour ago, amidst the glare and glitter of the Concert Hall. *Then,* the music had brought back only stinging memories; it had spoken to her of the joy that was gone for ever, of the peace and hope which could never come again. Now, it seemed to whisper of another home, even a heavenly; of a quiet soul rest, of a new and precious life where the past might be pardoned and the present calmed, and the future made, if not bright, at least peaceful and free from fear. As she listened, her heart grew still.

For awhile no one seemed inclined to break the holy silence which that music had left. Then a tall, sturdy, middle-aged man rose. He might be a carpenter, for he had a stoop in his shoulders and wore an apron tucked away round his waist under his coat. He was fresh and happy-looking.

He had a jovial face, lips that seemed to be always trying to hide a smile, and light, sunny, hazel eyes, with a certain twinkle of humour lurking in their clear, honest glance. He held his head well up, shaking back the hair, somewhat touched with grey, from his forehead. His accent was provincial in the extreme, but he spoke with an evident sense of enjoyment and hearty earnestness.

"Satan were tempting me as I came along," he began, "and says he to me, Luke Ryan, says he, you won't have nought to say when you get among all the folk. Ye'll be shamed while ye can't lift yer head up. Hould yer whisht, says I, I warn't ashamed to speak up right well i' your cause when I lived servant wi' you, an' its a poor story if I can't say a word for the Master what's done so much for me. It's a sorry sort o' shame, sir," and here he turned his face to the minister, "it's a sorry sort o' shame when folks can tongue away like mad i' the world's talk, and havn't a word to say for Him as bled for 'em. So I comed, though he tried hard, did the old fellow, to keep me back.

"Well, I'm always learnin'. I were an ould

scholar when I came into t' blessed Master's school, and says I to myself, Luke Ryan, says I, you mun be right sharp, 'cause the time is short, and death 'll be coming afore ye can spell out a chapter; and now things as I never looked to afore teaches me blessed lessons. If ye'd like to hear one or two on 'em I'll tell ye. T'other day I were off in t' country, puttin' up a barn door for a farmer as lives at Grassthorpe, an' afore I got there I took thirsty; it's a pretty far step to Grassthorpe, and though I don't go for to say nothin' agen the weather God Almighty sees fit to send—t' worst on it's better nor we deserve—it was one o' those reeky fixed up days as seems to take all a man's spring and spirit out on him. So I seed a pump nigh hand the toll-gate cottage, and off I set and began o' pumping. But t' pump nozzle were low, not over a span off t' ground, and I were forced to go down of my knees and stoop my head afore I could get a drop. Well, sir, that teached me a lesson. Says I to myself, Luke Ryan, says I, that there pump is like the Gospel of the Lord Jesus Christ. We must go down on our knees to it. It's when we're bowed in prayer and humility that the water of salvation comes pouring out and freshens the thirsty soul. But mind ye, if ye're over proud to stoop and put your lips to the pump nozzle, ye mun just go dry, an' serve ye right too. And I'm thinking, sir, this is the reason why babes and sucklings is oft more learned in the ways of God than us as thinks werselves summut great. They havn't so far to stoop. It don't go agen their nat'ral pride to kneel 'em down and drink. Bless us, what a glorious thing it 'ud be if we could all on us get the child-heart, and trust God Almighty, as a little bairn looks tull its father an' mother, never askin' no questions, but just goin' where He tells us to. I know the time when I wouldn't ha' said a prayer to save my soul. I glorified human natur over much, an' all t' time I was lean and dry, and withered as a bit o' kindlin'. A proud spirit and a poor heart, a proud spirit and a poor heart, that's the way it goes."

Luke's racy way of describing the dealings of God with his soul, seemed to cheer the people. It was as if a breeze of clear, fresh, healthy mountain air had swept over and chased away all of doubt and sadness that anyone might have brought into that little meeting. Even Mrs. Edenall raised her head, and a look of infinite longing and tenderness came stealing into her erewhile despairing face. The minister stood leaning over the desk, his arms folded upon it, a smile, which he did not attempt to restrain, coming and going upon his lips.

"And then, sir," continued Luke, "there's another thing I should like to say. I always look to get a good meal of speritle meat and drink first thing of a mornin', it makes me as fresh as a lark all the day. Folks as works hard, wants a good breakfast, and it ain't no yield trying to get on without it. And it's same with God Almighty's labourers, they mun get a good feed o' speritle meat and drink afore they set to work. I always gets up thick end of an hour afore the rest wakes, and has a clear still time readin' and meditatin', and bless ye, the good it does me, I can't tell. Mebby ye think it's time I were sittin' down now, but there's just one more thing strikes me, and when I've got it said, I won't talk no longer. Ye see I'm finding my tongue, friends, though Satan telled me I shouldn't ha' nought to say; but sometimes thoughts nestles in my mind as thick as sparrows in a cherry-tree, and I'm clean beat to find words to match 'em. Some folks has a gift o' thinkin' without talkin', and other folks has a gift o' talkin' without thinkin'. Now them's best off as gets a little o' both, and I believe that's way wi' me. Christian people now-a-days has got dainty appetites, plain food don't suit 'em no longer, they must have cakes and candy, and all manner o' things as ain't got no support in 'em. Now when I was a 'prentice lad, I ate plain food, lots o' meat and lots o' potaties, and lots o' good brown bread, but nowt else to speak on. And I throve well and pushed up'ards, and pushed out'ards, like yon elm trees i' the Close, till I got as big as ye see me now."

And Luke threw out his broad chest, and tossed back the hair from his sunburnt forehead—a veritable specimen of the best sort of muscular Christianity.

"Well friends," he continued, "that rule works both ways. Plain food's best for Christians. There's a vast o' what I call goody shops i' these times—high edicated men as preaches nought but fine larnin' an' pretty bits o' poetry an' sentences as finishes up with a flourish, as always reminds me of the city bellman, when he's gived out a notice, and tucks his bell under his arm wi' such an air as if there warn't another bell in England to match it. Well, folks listens to this sort o' preaching, and listens and listens and gets their mouths so full of sugar, while they can't relish things as has proper nutriment in 'em, the solid food o' the Gospel. Now I don't go to say nothing against fine preachers, them as sells goodies, ye know. I like a lozenge myself now and then for a change, but it won't do to keep to 'em, friends, it won't do to keep to 'em. We must come back to the old shop after all, and feed on the unleavened bread of sincerity and truth. And now I don't know that I've got anything else to say. God has been blessing my soul this week. As sister Cromarty says, He fills me often with such a holy joy, while I can't find words to tell it. And I love to work for Him, I never lets a day pass without speakin' a word for the Saviour, and trying to bring poor sinners to Him. May He bless us all, and keep us going right straight on to the end, and then say to us, 'Well done good and faithful servants.' Amen!"

Before Luke Ryan had finished, the hour-hand of the clock pointed to ten. Again the minister rose and gave out a hymn, which was sung to one of those hearty, energetic, inspiring tunes the Primitive Methodists love so well. Everyone joined in it. Even the old man who had that week buried his dead out of his sight, tuned up, and in a faint, quavering voice tried to swell the chorus.

"Let us pray," said the minister, when the hymn was over. Again they knelt, and he offered another short prayer, to which the people responded as before. He asked that God would bless the word spoken that night; that He would help those present to go through their work with fresh energy, doing all they did as unto God, and not unto man; seeing in every duty a means of grace, and brightening every trial with the hope of glory which lay beyond. He asked that wherever Christ's people saw the print of their Master's footsteps, they might be willing to place their own, even though thorns were in the track. He asked that the weary and heavy-laden might go away from that meeting refreshed, that the tempted might be strengthened, that the brother on whom God had laid His afflicting hand might have the oil and wine of heavenly grace richly poured into his heart; and that all sorrow, where-ever sent, might yield hereafter the peaceable fruit of righteousness.

Listening to him, Mrs. Edenall felt, for the first time in her life, how strongly through such prayers as these—

"The whole round world is every way
Bound by gold chains about the feet of God."

The people seemed in no hurry to leave after the service was over. Some of them clustered together, talking over the words that had been said. The minister went about amongst them, speaking good words, pleasant words too they seemed to be, from the bright looks which they called forth. He stayed long by the side of the old man, holding his withered hand, and speaking to him in gentle tender tones.

Mrs. Edenall lingered until nearly the last. She would have stolen away unperceived if she could, but the preacher saw her just as she was going out.

"Madam," he said, laying his hand on hers,

which were clasped so tightly beneath the folds of her cloak. "Madam, you are a stranger to me, but I trust we are both members of that family which shall one day meet unbroken before the throne of God."

The words were very simple, but they went to her heart. He said them with a grave sweet tenderness, smiling all the while. She could not reply, for his kindness had brought the tears to her eyes. She glided silently past him into the quiet, dimly-lighted street, and he saw her no more. It was the last service he ever held in that room. The next Thursday evening a stranger was in his place, the next he was worshipping in the temple not made with hands.

This was one of those chance meetings, burdened sometimes with the issues of life or death, wherein for one brief moment heart touches heart beneath the shadow of God's presence, and in that touch finds healing.

CHAPTER XIX.

ALL this time Janet and David sat quietly together in the parlour at Westwood. For once she had laid aside the little white sock, and was hemming a fine cambric pocket-handkerchief for her brother. A pair of white gloves lay on the work-table by her side, she had been stitching the buttons more securely on—Janet had an almost idolatrous reverence for her brother's comfort in the matter of buttons—and beside the gloves was a black silk tie which required an inch of its length curtailing.

Janet Bruce looked peaceful, almost happy, as she stitched away with the regularity and precision of a sewing machine. This sisterly love, in all its patient and sometimes scarcely noticed ministrations, was the only earthly interest left to fill and quiet her life.

David Bruce had been working hard through the day, and seemed weary enough when Janet took away his overcoat and helped him on with the loose study wrap of fine tartan which had been warming at the fire for an hour past. But it was only bodily weakness, his voice was cheery and genial, even breaking forth now and then into a low pleasant laugh, as by-and-by they began to talk of the old life with its cares and struggles over-past,—of the coming life too, brightened in Janet's thoughts by the stillness of unbroken home-peace, in David's by hopes too bright to be steadily gazed upon until now.

Janet never dreamed of her brother marrying. He was so silent and reserved, so completely unlike the trim, dapper, finely polished men, who prove most successful in matrimonial speculations. Even in the days of their prosperity at Perth, when, had he been so disposed, he might have "settled advantageously," as the phrase is, he had led a quiet shut-up life, never entangled in anything that had the remotest tinge of romance or love-making; and since the sudden stroke which swept away their fortune and compelled them to begin the world afresh, the struggle for daily bread had been so uncertain, that she was quite sure he would be far too proud to ask any woman to share it with him. She never asked herself how she should feel if another chanced to come in between them, and take from her hands those loving little duties which it had so long been the sweetness of her life to offer; nor how her lips would learn to fashion another phrase than the one so habitual to them now—"My brother and I."

The sleet drove heavily against the windows, and the leafless branches of the linden trees creaked as the wind chafed upon them; but the brother and sister by their cosy fireside heard neither. They did not often get a quiet evening together now. Ever since David's return from London, three weeks ago, the strange nervous excitability which had come over Mrs. Edenall had sadly marred their household peace. Janet was utterly perplexed to account for this change. Mrs. Edenall had received no letters that could have troubled her, for it was months now since any bearing her name had been left at Westwood; nor did she seem to be fretting herself over their non-arrival, for the postman's knock never startled her, she never wearied for his coming, nor seemed disappointed as morning after morning he passed by the garden gate. She would own to no illness, indeed she seemed to scorn all bodily fatigue and exposure, and would tramp through the wildest storms, or over miles of snow-covered moorland, with a proud angry sort of defiance. It could not be either that she was chafed by any seeming neglect of her comfort, for all the household arrangements were carried on in the old way, and never by the slightest hint was she made aware that her presence was less needed than heretofore. Yet day by day she became more incomprehensible. She was her old self again, nay, worse than her old self, for the Mrs. Edenall of eight months ago was only cold and haughtily indifferent, and the Mrs. Edenall of the last few weeks had been like a perpetual presence of evil in the quiet little household.

As the time of the Festival drew on, she seemed to be possessed with an uncontrollable spirit of restlessness. When she was not pacing rapidly up and down the room, her fingers would twitch nervously, and anything that she took into her hands was soon pulled to pieces. Sometimes she used to sit for hours together, tearing up paper into small fragments with the desperate sort of industry of a person who puts her whole soul into the work, her lips trembling all the while and her forehead gathered into frowns. Then she would lay them on the hot bars of the fireplace and watch with a sardonic smile how they withered and curled and shrivelled before the hissing flames leaped forth upon them.

A chilling fear came into Janet's mind sometimes that the woman was really becoming mad; only that her thoughts when she did converse were always quite collected, and when she argued on any subject with Mr. Bruce—which she often did, for it seemed to afford a vent for the latent combativeness of her nature—there was a clear, forceful energy and foresightedness in all she said. Still Janet seemed more and more to shrink from her. Only the incident of Mrs. Edenall's great kindness during those dreary weeks of illness lingered on, and could not beforgotten.

But though neither of them made any complaint, both felt that it was pleasant to have the little spell of quiet which her absence afforded. It seemed when she was gone as if some strange inexplicable bond had suddenly been lifted away from them, as if the passes of some invisible hand had ceased, and its magnetic current stayed.

David Bruce's prosperity so far had made no difference to the establishment at Westwood.

Everything went on in the old-fashioned track under Tibbie's active management. At the time prescribed by etiquette, Miss Bruce put on her seldom-worn black silk dress and made a round of calls; but the dinner, supper, and quadrille party invitations which speedily followed were all declined, and so the sudden explosion of friendliness on the part of the Close families seemed likely to end in smoke. Looking in upon the two as they sat there so easily and quietly, he in his great arm chair, she in a low Devonshire seat by his side, it seemed likely enough to remain "my brother and I" to the end of the chapter.

"There then, Davie, it is finished," said Janet,

holding up the silken-fine handkerchief between her eyes and the lamplight. "Now I'll mark it in commemoration of the occasion."

She fetched a little bottle of marking ink from the closet and began very slowly to write upon the corner. Then she held it to the fire, which brought out in small dainty characters the inscription—

"David Bruce. Westwood parlour. The night before the Oratorio."

"Now, Davie," she said, as she flung it playfully over his face—Janet was quite in an exalted state of merriment to-night—"there won't be a finer handkerchief than that in the Hall of Guild to-morrow night, and so if your feelings overcome you, you needn't be ashamed of giving way to them, and letting it have a baptism of tears. I believe everything is quite ready now. I have fastened those buttons of yours securely —it's so disagreeable, you know, when they come off just at the last moment—and that necktie is exactly the length you want. And Davie, now, do mind when you go to dress what collar you get out of the box. I should be so concerned if I saw you come on the orchestra with one of those untidy Napoleons, like what you are wearing now."

"Never mind, Jeanie, they're very comfortable, but I'll do as you tell me if I can remember."

David Bruce said no more. Just then a gleam of firelight wandering over his study wrap, shone upon a single golden hair, a long, waving, rippling golden hair, which had lain undisturbed ever since that November afternoon when Alice Grey came to say good-bye to him before he went to London. Then, such a weary distance seemed to part them. Heart to heart though they stood, the iron barriers of caste gloomed grimly up between them and kept the hands asunder which belonged to each other. Now they stood free and equal, and those fingers of hers would not soil their high-born whiteness within the clasp of his. It was this thought that made the rare smile flash like sunshine over his face.

Janet noted the smile, but nothing more. Seeing that he did not seem inclined to talk, she took up the knitting work that lay upon the table, and presently fell into a train of meditation which blossomed out after the lapse of a full half-hour into speech.

"Davie, I have been thinking that now money matters are so much easier with us than they used to be, I can make you a set of real fine linen shirts. I have been wanting you to have them so long, all linen you know, like what you used to wear in the old times. And, Davie, perhaps after this Oratorio, you'll be obliged to go a little more into company, and I thought a couple of them had better be made with a tiny little cambric frill and a strip of embroidery down the fronts, for full dress you know."

No answer, not even a smile from those still shut-up lips.

The mention of visiting seemed to lead Janet's thoughts to the Old Lodge, the only home whose hospitality they had shared since their residence in St. Olave's, for by-and-by she said—

"Alice Grey comes home to-night."

David turned round with a questioning look.

"Alice Grey comes home to-night, Davie," and then Janet paused to pick up a stitch that had slipped from the needle.

It was almost the only time Alice's name had been mentioned since that evening of David's return from London. Somehow she had not been to

Westwood so frequently of late. Mr. Bruce's long illness necessarily slacked their intercourse; then close upon it came Aunt Amiel's affliction and Alice's visit to Brighton, not to mention that new interest which had sprung up in her life and made other friendships less needful. As for David, the thought of her lay too far away down in his heart ever to come up with the stray drift that sometimes floated to the surface.

"Yes, she was to arrive about eight o'clock. Miss Luckie told me. And, brother, it has been on my mind a long time to ask her to tea. You know we ought to have done so after the pic-nic last September, but your going to London interfered, and I thought she might not care so much to come when you were away, for she likes to hear you talk and listen to your music. She told me once she liked your music better than any other."

Still, no answer but the smile, the deepening smile which Janet loved so well to see upon her brother's face, for it seemed to speak to her of rest after the hard toil and struggle of the past few years. David had been so grave since they came to St. Olave's. She went on.

"I know Alice is very fond of coming here,

but Mrs. Edenall is so strange just now that she might not enjoy it so much. You might play to her though in the front parlour, and I could keep Mrs. Edenall here. I am sure she would be glad to come. She told me a long time ago that she was looking forward to this Festival very much, and I believe it was because she thought your Oratorio would likely be performed."

Janet said all this, knitting on in her quiet, peaceful, unconscious way, looking sometimes into the clear firelight, sometimes into her brother's face, with that staid unquestioning expression that had become so habitual to her.

What a comfort it is sometimes to be talked to by people of slow comprehension, people who don't have "intuitions" or "impressions" or "presentiments,"—people who have not learned to use that magic elixir which, poured over the tablets of the heart, brings out the hidden writing upon them. Janet Bruce was singularly unperceptive. She never found out a truth for herself, and even when one was presented to her, she rarely received it except after very patient investigation. Her processes of thought were slow, deliberate, lengthy.

And yet she was a great comfort to her

brother, more so perhaps than if had she been one of those inventive geniuses who can divine the destinies of a lifetime from the glance of an eye or the lightning of a momentary smile.

When Alice made that little speech about the Festival, it was with an innocent hope that the remark might produce further questioning, and so give her an opportunity of disclosing the secret with which her young heart was burdened. But Janet had not perceived this, and so as yet she remained in ignorance of Alice Grey's engagement.

She was not likely to hear of it in any other way.

The etiquette of courtship, especially in its earlier stages, was somewhat rigid amongst the Close families.

Those arm-in-arm strolls and moonlight *tête-a-têtes*, whereby young people of the middle classes proclaim their mutual attachment, were frowned upon by the St. Olave's upper ten, and monopolized by scullery girls or maids of all work. Not until the marriage-day was fixed and the bridal outfit prepared was it considered correct for affianced aristocrats to make a public appearance in each other's company. So that as yet gossip had not laid its smutty finger on Alice's name to link it with that of her future husband ; nor, had Miss Bruce possessed the *entrée* of all the St. Olave's tea-circles, would she have been enlightened as to the matrimonial prospects of her young friend. Perhaps the closeness of the Close people in this respect was very wise.

Janet was still talking to her brother when the garden gate opened, and footsteps were heard on the gravel walk. Their pleasant evening was at an end. No, not quite, for Mrs. Edenall passed the parlour and went up-stairs to her own room, not even coming in to say the good-night and give the parting hand-clasp which had been exchanged so often between them.

Janet heaved a little sigh of relief and settled down to the knitting work again, as the door of Mrs. Edenall's room closed and the grating of the key in the lock sounded through the wide passage.

"Surely the concert cannot be through yet, Davie; but she's been aye restless the day, and perhaps she was wearying for home."

CHAPTER XX.

IT was the last day of the Festival. Since Monday the excitement had been thickening; and indeed it was time the great affair came to a crisis, for St. Olave's had been turned wrong side out, upside down, and downside up, until the poor little city scarce knew itself for the same. The Cathedral bells had rung themselves hoarse. Morning, noon, and night their clamour smote upon the air. The rooks in the belfry tower were well nigh distracted, and after bearing the nuisance for a day or two had retired in disgust to temporary lodgings within the Westwood elms. Indeed, had the hubbub continued much longer, they must have presented themselves in a body to the Dean and Chapter to pray for a restoration of peace.

For the first three days, multitudes of cheap-trippers had flaunted through the streets, brandishing cotton umbrellas and carrying huge baskets of prog with bottle necks protruding through the lids. Even the Cathedral pavement itself had been defaced by remains of penny pies and wrappings of ham sandwiches, for the Millsmany folk turned the nave into a temporary symposium, and gratified their organs of admiration and alimentiveness simultaneously.

Friday, however, the great day of the Festival, was set apart for the exclusive benefit of the county families. The last of the cheap trips had cleared away out of the station. The vulgar tones of the mill people no longer mingled like a muddy torrent with the clear silvery ringing accents of the "quality." The lower stratum of the social compact had had its share of enjoyment, and this closing evening was sacred to "Jael" and gentility.

Alice Grey and Mrs. Scrymgeour arrived from Brighton on Thursday. She was to go to the Oratorio with the party from Chapter Court; Mrs.

Cromarty promised to take exclusive charge of Aunt Amiel for one evening, in order that Miss Luckie might chaperon Janet Bruce, for David expected to be hard at work up to the very last moment.

The St. Olave's Hall of Guild, where the musical festivals were held, was a noble old place, in thorough keeping with the rest of the city. It was erected by the burghers in the sixteenth century, and its massy walls had looked upon many a jovial banquet in the merry days of yore. Since the completion of the new Mansion-house it had been disused for civic purposes, and the Corporation fitted it up as a public room for concerts, assemblies, and the like. It was a long lofty building, with a richly-carved and groined roof. Formerly the space between the groining was left plain, but after its appropriation as a Music Hall, it was decorated with rich arabesque tracery of crimson, blue, and gold, and lit by innumerable tiny jets of gas that threw out into fine relief its quaint old bosses and finely wrought medallions. The windows were mullioned, filled with stained glass, which in the day time gave the room quite an ecclesiastical appearance. On full-dress occasions, however, they were draped by heavy crimson velvet curtains, which formed an effective background for the ladies' brightly tinted costumes. The spaces between the windows were filled in with a diaper pattern of blue and gold, with heraldic devices belonging to the different families of St. Olave's. Here and there a scarred and tattered banner, relic of some long-past battle, fluttered from the groined roof, strangely out of character with the present appearance of the place, but telling its own story of rack and tumult.

The orchestra was very beautiful, occupying one entire end of the room. It was enclosed by three lofty arches springing from clustered columns, and rising to the roof. Within these arches, high up out of sight, were placed rows of lights pouring down a rich glow upon the organ, which with its elaborately decorated pipes looked like some gorgeous Eastern shrine or Moorish mosque.

Round the back of this orchestra, in deep stone niches with canopies carved and fretted like those of the Cathedral, were ranged the statues of Europe's great composers. Handel, the melodious Titan, massive and majestic as one of his own choruses; Beethoven, the Michael Angelo of music, with his sublime brow and tangled elf locks; Weber, pale, passionless, and still, pure as an iceberg, and as cold; Mendelssohn, with that uplifted heaven-lighted face of his,—living so near to the angels what wonder he caught their likeness? Mozart, upon whose calm front, fame and death so early set their seal, was there too; and Haydn, with clasped hands and lips folded down in stately repose. Pergolesi bent forward his rapt face as though listening to far-off choirs; Rossini, bright and jubilant as a strain of Italian song, smiled his everlasting smile; and next him came Bellini, quiet and self-contained as his own Norma, yet not lacking the mingled grace and sweetness which could conceive the wondrous melodies of Somnambula. Nor in that guild of fame-crowned heads were wanting those whom England has nurtured, and whose names have helped to make her famous. Tallis, Bird, Purcell, Gibbon, Farrant, staunch venerable old patron saints of music, whose grand thoughts, breathed forth day by day from many a Cathedral choir, keep their name and memory green, uplifted their heads side by side with the great continental *maestros;* the quaint, trim nationality of their aspect contrasting oddly, and yet not unpleasantly, with the laurel-wreathed brows and flowing robes of their foreign compeers.

The hall filled; group after group of gaily-dressed people came sailing in. Stout old squiresses in purple velvet and diamonds; blonde beauties in clouds of floating tulle; here and there a bride—there had been some weddings lately amongst the county families—half-hidden in a snow-drift of white *glacé;* then a brunette, resplendent in crimson draperies, or magnificently flashing in amber satin and black lace. One by one, the military people, always a great feature in St. Olave's on public occasions, came dropping in, their laced and braided uniforms flashing back the glare of light from the roof.

Amongst the earliest arrivals came Mrs. Archdeacon Scrymgeour, in a strong-minded looking dress of some dead black material, over which a transparent scarf of greyish-white gauze meandered, like puffs of steam from an unpolished tea-kettle. Cuthbert Scrymgeour and Alice accompanied her—I speak advisedly; the Archdeacon's widow never, in the social sense of the word, condescended to *accompany* her friends she was always *the* circumstance of any group in which she formed a part, the active inflection of the verb. Alice wore a white dress to-night, the same as that in which she had appeared at the eventful Chapter Court party, only that now her delicate beauty was heightened by an opera mantle of light blue, edged with miniver, and, instead of the pearl cordon, one single half-blown white rose was placed in her hair, nestling lovingly amongst the brown curls, as though glad to find so pleasant a resting-place.

Blanche Egerton, the dreamy-eyed brunette, came in next, bland, regal, composed, leaning on the arm of the county member. His other convenience for escorting ladies was occupied by Miss Fullerton, who seemed to view the whole concern from a metropolitan point of view, and despised it accordingly. After them, Captain Madden brought in the two Misses Spurge, with their mamma in the background—a turbulent mass of satin, pearls, and flounces. Next came Janet Bruce and Miss Luckie; but, as their appearance did not add to the brilliance of the scene, it is needless to particularize them. There was a very gay party from the Palace; the Bishop himself could not be present on account of his duties at the House; but the Honourable Mrs. Standish, with half a dozen guests, more than supplied his place. The Deanery contributed its quota of beauty, in the shape of Elene Somers and her cousin, blonde nymphs in blue and silver, attended by a major from the barracks. After them came Canon Crumpet and his lady, bringing up the rear of the Close phalanx ecclesiastical.

As the Cathedral bells struck eight, the band and chorus took their places, to the number of nearly a hundred. For the most part, they were a noble-looking set, with the frank, open expression of countenance which men, whose life employment is a joy to them, generally wear. Following them, were the little chorister boys from the Cathedral, with carefully-polished faces and well-brushed hair. The little fellows looked very solemn, and were evidently perplexed about the management of their hands—a perplexity which ended by the unruly members being pocketed.

When all was arranged, David Bruce, holding his roll of music and conductor's baton, came up the narrow stair that led from the private room. A tumultuous sound of applause greeted him as he stood for a moment or two in front of the orchestra, before taking his place at the desk. He received it very calmly, not appearing either pleased or flattered by it. There was a sort of rock-like firmness about his character, against which the waves of praise and blame alike might beat as long as they chose, and move it not a hair's-breadth.

Janet Bruce was very humble. There was not a particle of what the world calls vanity or conceit in her composition; but a flush of pleasure eddied up to her forehead, as she saw her brother receiving the homage and admiration of a set of people who, six months ago, would have scorned to give him even the honour of a passing smile. She thought he looked very noble, kingly as any king might look, as he acknowledged, with a certain grave, sedate majesty, the greetings flung upon him. The light shone bravely down over his grand face, so calm, so almost proud in its stillness, and threw out, in bold relief against the crimson draperies of the orchestra, his great massive head, with its crown of tangled hair.

For one brief moment he scanned that sea of upturned faces, searching for the one which day and night lay ever in his thoughts. He found it; their eyes met, and a bright smile of recognition flashed from hers. David Bruce bent his head to hide the eager flush of pleasure which that look had brought, then turned away to his place at the conductor's desk.

By the rules of the Festival Committee, applause of any kind during the performance of sacred music was strictly forbidden; and, when the first peals of welcome had subsided, the Oratorio proceeded in the midst of profound silence. But there needed neither waving of handkerchiefs nor clapping of hands to show how surely it was winning its way to the hearts of the people. It was strange to notice how, even before the overture came to a close, the professionals, who were in the room, bent forward with keen interest, and then one by one moved, as if drawn by some invisible magnet, to the front of the orchestra, where they stood with clasped hands and rapt, wondering faces. Again and again, as the last notes of some exquisite chorale or solo died away, a sigh of intense excitement thrilled through the room, and a low murmur of delight, stifled as soon as it broke forth by the quick, impatient "Hush! hush!" of eager listeners.

Smiles chased over Alice's face, as she recognized phrase after phrase of music that she had copied for him, or which David had played to her in the little parlour at Westwood. On the music swept; sometimes grand and stately, with a strong, over-mastering force, beneath which the whole concourse of people swayed hither and thither, like reeds shaken by the wind; sometimes plaintive and weird-like, waking hearts that had long time slept, and raising them, as all true music does, to a purer life. Many bowed their faces and wept; some with shut eyes listened, not to the music, but to the memories it had stirred within them; and a few men and women, whom the angel Gabriel might have tried in vain to move, just sat through it all with vacant, unsmiling faces.

David Bruce, standing with his back to the people, saw nothing of all this. His whole mind was intent on the work he had to do; and very nobly he did it. His countenance reflected each shade of feeling in the music; its spirit seemed to have entered into him, making his every gesture instinct with matchless grace and dignity. The performers, watching him eagerly, caught his enthusiasm, and obeyed, with deft skill, each motion of the magic baton, which, now uplifted, now depressed, swelled or curbed their harmonies.

After the close of the first part of the Oratorio, there was an interval of twenty minutes. The band and chorus speedily emptied themselves into the large ante-room below, where they fell to work upon the cold collation that had been provided there. For musicians, like other men, have "internal motives," and musical exertion, whether it be of throat or arms, appears to have an invigorating effect upon the appetite.

After the orchestra was cleared, the hall converted itself into a promenade. Gentlemen got up and sauntered about to stretch themselves after two hours' spell of unwonted excitement. The connoisseurs clustered into little groups here and there, eagerly discussing the merits of the music.

Miss Luckie, to whom even a silence of ten minutes seemed interminable, broke out into a pleasant little trickle of conversation as soon as the restraint was removed.

"So happy to congratulate you, my dear Miss

Bruce, so very happy. It really must be such a triumph to you. To think, you know, that Mr. Bruce, poor man—at least—oh dear I beg pardon! I'm always saying things I didn't mean to, but Mr. Bruce was such a quiet man, such an exceedingly quiet man, I remarked that from the very first, that no one ever supposed he would be likely to stand in such a position as he occupies to-night, and I'm sure if he were my own brother I couldn't be more glad for him, and for you too, dear Miss Bruce. But I do believe the Bishop's lady is coming this way to offer her congratulations; yes, she is indeed. I declare it has put me quite into a flutter. Don't introduce me, dear Miss Bruce, pray don't; my heart beats so I don't know what to do." And Miss Luckie's Nottingham lace lappets—she had got a new head dress for the occasion—whisked round in a perfect tremor of nervous agitation.

Yes, the Honourable Mrs. Standish's black velvet dress was actually sweeping the floor just in front of them, and her ostrich plumes swayed in the scented air as she reached out her gloved hand with calm cathedralesque dignity. She was proud to have the honour of felicitating Miss

Bruce on the brilliant success of the evening; the name of David Bruce would henceforth confer new honour on St. Olave's; she hoped this was only the commencement of a series of triumphs which should ere long elevate the illustrious composer to the highest pinnacle of musical fame, &c. &c. Ere Mrs Standish had concluded her flowery address, she made way for the Dean's lady and Sir Harry Monbello, who had come on the same errand; and they were followed by Canon Crumpet and the county member and his daughter. Indeed Miss Bruce held quite a miniature levee during that space of twenty minutes.

"Thank you, you are kind," was the only answer she could make to the compliments and congratulations which poured down upon her. Poor Janet, she had a very limited stock of the sugared bon-bons of social intercourse. She never said anything that she did not mean, and people who make much of sincerity soon get stranded in their conversational cruises.

By-and-by Alice came.

"I couldn't press my way through the fence of aristocracy before," she said, nestling her hand in Janet's whilst her eyes sparkled and her face flushed with pleasure, "but I'm glad for you Miss Bruce, I'm very glad."

It was all she said; a half quiver in her voice told the rest.

"How sweet Miss Grey is looking to-night," said Janet as Alice floated away to her seat beside Mrs. Scrymgeour, Cuthbert was in another part of the room talking to some gentlemen friends; "I think she grows prettier and prettier."

"Yes, yes," replied Miss Luckie with a series of pleasant mysterious little nods, "won't it be a very delightful sight now to see her in her veil and orange blossom?"

"Well I suppose it will. Is there a possibility of her appearing in that costume before long?"

"Why you know," and Miss Luckie dropped her voice and went through another series of nods, "it isn't talked about yet, but I don't mind telling you because I know you live so very retired and won't mention it again; I do believe Miss Bruce, if I were to get married myself, the wedding dress would have been dyed and turned bottom to the top before you would hear of the affair. Yes, I am happy to say Alice has achieved her destiny; at least she has taken the preliminary steps. You know I'm always so glad when young people get engaged, it's so much better than hanging on the bough until they get quite out of season and then drop off into irretrievable old maidenhood."

"And may I ask who the gentleman is?" said Janet, with that faintest little tinge of curiosity which creeps unawares into every woman's heart at the mention of a wedding.

"Dear me, how stupid not to have told you that at first, but I never could get into the way of saying the right thing at the right time. The fortunate individual is Mr. Scrymgeour, the nephew of the Archdeacon's widow, you know. There he is, look, sitting beside her,—no he isn't either; really now where can he have got to, I'm sure he was there not ten minutes ago—Oh! yonder he is, standing just under the second window, you see him, don't you, with curly hair and long whiskers?"

"Yes. I am not surprised, Mr Scrymgeour is very handsome," and Janet's thoughts went back to the evening of the pic-nic when she and David had touched upon that same subject. It had always seemed to her likely enough that Alice should take a fancy to Mr. Scrymgeour.

"You think he is handsome, don't you? I said

when first he began to come about the house that he was a perfect—dear me, what do they call that good looking god?—Apollo, ah that's it. I always said he was a perfect Apollo, just the sort of young man you know to fascinate a girl of good taste, and such perfect manners. The wedding is to be this summer."

"I do not know him at all, except by sight. But they will be a striking pair."

"You're quite right. It isn't often that beautiful women are equally matched in that respect. A very pretty girl I once knew, fixed her affections on the oddest piece of humanity that was ever invented, and turned him into a husband. A very good one he made too—everybody said the match was a perfectly happy one; but I always think it's a pity for such things to happen."

"The only thing that troubles me," continued Miss Luckie, who seemed loth to quit her subject, "the only thing that troubles me is, that I am afraid we can't have anything much of a spread at the wedding. You see poor dear old Mrs. Grey's terrible state of health quite precludes any attempt at splendour. And I do so dote on a pretty wedding. From such a magnificent old house too. Do you know there hasn't been a wedding from the Lodge for ninety years, and it would have rejoiced my heart to have seen everything in first-rate style. I expect Mrs. Scrymgeour will have the management, and I shall feel quite distressed if the occasion passes off with anything less than eight bridesmaids and a moire antique. But, dear me, I declare the band is coming back again; how soon the time slips away when one is chatting."

The orchestra filed into their places, and the music was resumed. The people listened with unabated, or, if possible, intenser interest. There was more of dramatic excitement in the second part of the Oratorio. Jael's deed of desperate daring, Deborah's triumphant ode, the dirge of the childless mother, and the jubilant chorus of a freed nation—these were grand subjects for a musician, and David had dealt nobly with them.

Scarcely were the last lingering tones of the concluding chorus hushed, when the pent-up enthusiasm of the people burst forth in acclamations, which seemed as if they would shake the building down. Surely never before had the good folks of St. Olave's allowed themselves to be so carried away by their feelings. Hats and handkerchiefs were waved, bouquets were thrown upon the orchestra—even staid old Cathedral dignitaries shared in the general excitement, and helped forward the applause with feet, hands, and voices. Thrice that night was David Bruce recalled upon the orchestra; and thrice, as he obeyed the summons, peals of greeting made the echoes of the old room ring again, and shook the air until the shot-torn banners that had hung motionless for centuries, quivered in every fold.

David Bruce stood very calmly amidst it all.

They had but given him his own place, and crowned him with the laurels his own toil had won. And those laurels were only dear to him because, wearing them, he might stand worthily side by side with Alice Grey.

When the tumult had somewhat ceased, he made his way down into the little private room behind the orchestra. Not private now though, for it was thronged with *dilettanti* noblemen and connoisseurs, who had come to congratulate the composer on his brilliant success. And dainty, white-gloved hands were held out for a touch of his, and there was a sheen of satin and flutter of lace as one courtly dame after another pressed forwards to solicit an introduction; and eyes that had erewhile turned scornfully away looked brightly into his, and lips once curled in contempt wore a smile most sweet and humble.

It was David Bruce's coronation night—he stood a king amongst them at last.

An hour later, he and Janet sat quietly together in the little parlour at Westwood. He was very pale and worn, but there was a happy smile upon his face—the smile of one who has toiled and triumphed, and rests now in the consciousness of victory. Janet sat by him, still in the dress she had worn at the Hall of Guild—black silk, with a single deep red rose that David had given her, fastened into the velvet knot which covered her hair behind. The most fastidious critic would scarcely have called Janet Bruce plain to-night for the pride of a loving heart shone through her face, and that makes any one beautiful.

David would not have the lamp lighted, so they sat there in the clear red fire-light, he leaning back wearily in his great arm-chair. They were talking of his long waiting time, and the success which had crowned it at last. And as very often when they were alone, they journeyed back again to the long-ago Perth days, to the old, old life which, behind this sudden sunshine of prosperity, seemed slipping farther and farther away. At last the talk wore itself out. Janet folded her hands on her knees and sent forward, gazing dreamily into the fire. David turned his head away from her, dreaming too.

Was it dreamlight or firelight that brightened all his face? Let him dream on, the waking will come in its own time and its own way.

The Minster bell struck one—a solitary sharp sound falling heavily upon the silence that had grown so deep between them. Janet heard it, and roused herself as if suddenly remembering something.

"Brother Davie, wake up."

"I was no asleep, Jean—only thinking."

"Well, then, I have got a piece of news to tell you."

"A piece of news! It is not often you happen on such a precious commodity. What is it about?"

"I suppose you mean *who* is it about. Our little friend Alice Grey is going to be married."

David Bruce said nothing. His head drooped a little lower, that was all.

"Now, Davie, don't go to sleep again, until I get it all told. You know Mr. Scrymgeour—Mr. Cuthbert Scrymgeour—that very handsome gentleman with the long whiskers—the same, indeed, who brought Alice home from the pic-nic that night—well, she is going to marry him, and the wedding is to be this summer. I told you once that I thought as much: but you did not believe me. Won't she make a bonnie bride?"

"*Janet!*"

The voice startled her, it was so changed. He turned his face; its utter paleness, and the awful cramp of agony which had come into it, told her all.

"Davie, brother Davie; I did not know. I never thought of this."

"Hush, Janet—don't speak."

He leaned his cheek down upon her hand in the old tender way as she drew closer to him. Presently, she bent her head softly over his, and put her arm round him. But she spoke no word, for she knew that it was the valley of the shadow of death through which he was passing.

So, for another hour they sat, not a sigh, not a movement, breaking the stillness of that terrible vigil. At last, he raised his face; his sister could scarcely bear to look upon it.

"Janet," he said, "I never told her anything. She has done me no wrong. I am sair weary now. Good night."

He stooped down and kissed her. His hands were damp and trembling, and the lips which touched her own quite cold. So they parted, and that was the last time for many and many a day that the name of Alice Grey was spoken between them.

END OF VOL. II.

CPSIA information can be obtained
at www.ICGtesting.com
Printed in the USA
LVHW040435110522
718423LV00002B/325

9 783375 001940